The Great Movie Robbery

by

R.L. Benwitt

Copyright © 2001 by R.L. Benwitt

ISBN 0-7414-0651-9

Cover design by Christopher A. Master
Published by:

Infinity Publishing.com
519 West Lancaster Avenue
Haverford, PA 19041-1413
Info@buybooksontheweb.com
www.buybooksontheweb.com
Toll-free (877) BUY BOOK
Local Phone (610) 520-2500
Fax (610) 519-0261

Printed in the United States of America

Printed on Recycled Paper

Published June, 2001

Dedication

This book and anything else I may accomplish in life is dedicated to my wife Connie for her years of love, friendship and uncompromising stability and emotional support.

Whatever career path, and there have been several over the last 28 years I decided to follow, her only comment was always an unqualified, "Go for it!"

A woman with a backbone of steel in the body of an American Beauty Rose, with the heart of a benevolent Queen. A fine example of American royalty.

Acknowledgements

Kent Carroll, our friend, without whom this book would not have been written. He not only encouraged me to write but taught me a great deal about the subject. A man who clearly would make one hell of a professor of Journalism at any university with serious minded students.

Who one night in our favorite neighborhood pub popped up with the notion that, "wouldn't it be funny if someone mounted a movie company to…" a comment that became the genesis for this book.

Kent's humility, not my time or lack of appreciation, prevents me from going on about the many other manifestations of his gracious and generous support to Connie and me over the years.

In addition, as one of the worlds preeminent book editors on two continents, his most recent help was in editing this book. It's better because of his efforts. Suffice it to say, if you have only one friend, it need only be Kent.

Jodee Blanco, President of Blanco & Peace Public Relations, Chicago without whom this book would not have been published. I could not resist a plug for her company. Simply and emphatically, without her, this book would still be in a manuscript box under my bed. It was her friendship and initiative that brought my manuscript to the publisher.

Listed alphabetically are others whom I wish to acknowledge for their friendship and support.

Colonel F. Patrick Ahearn, USMCR, for including us in many patriotic ceremonies and events. And for his tenacious efforts on my behalf with the Navy community.

Andy Garguilo, for his encouragement after reading my manuscript and sending it to everyone he thought might help. Comments from some of those gave me the impetus to continue the search for a publisher.

John Ginocchio, a good friend in every sense of the word for over 30 years. One who always believed, that in spite of my many career turns, I would someday be published. However, most significantly, made sure I got to the church on time for my wedding 28 years ago.

CDR Craig Himel, USN (Ret.) For getting me home from the hospital and, other things, not the least of which, was Army Navy football tickets.

SSGT Alex Kitsakos, USMCR, for so often going out of his way to accommodate us.

Frank and Marge Kraus, for all that they have done for my family over the years.

Wayne S. Marshall, PhD, supportive and encouraging in every sense of the words for the last three decades.

CDR Charlene Reim, USCGR, for getting me to a hospital and other acts of support since that trying time.

Captain Alan R. Rinando, USNR (Ret.) for bringing me on board the Naval Coastal Warfare News Magazine and his efforts for my advancement within the Coast Guard community.

CHAPTER ONE

If it weren't for the guard at the door, the prison library could be mistaken for one in a big Wall Street law firm.

Ziggey "The Z Man" Zignorelli, was seated opposite Mr. Yoshi at a small, dimly lit corner table. Ziggey was more chewing than smoking a cheap cigar, Mr. Yoshi was savoring a Dunhill 100 cigarette, held between his thumb and forefinger European style. On the small table lamp between two upholstered chairs were the signs of wealth. Next to the gold nugget Dunhill cigarette lighter and gold cigarette case was a half empty liter of Glen Fiddich Scotch. And judging from the body posture and slurred speech, that half bottle had been recently emptied by Mr. Yoshi. "The Z Man" was nursing a Coke.

The contrast between these two went far beyond their choices in tobacco and drinks. Mr. Yoshi was an imposing Japanese gentleman, dressed impeccably in Brooks Brothers Made to Measure, who spoke, when sober, perfect Oxford English.

The "Z" man, on the other hand, well, it helped if you were from the streets of New York to understand the slang, bad grammar and other very localized expressions. As for clothes, Ziggey didn't give a damn. Pants, shirt, shoes and not always socks were applied to his five foot seven inch body with no apparent concern as to color or condition.

So why were these two unlikely types together, particularly since there were others in this country club prison who represented more likely pairings? The answer was simple: Ziggey was working. He was working Mr. Yoshi for information. Any information he might someday find useful in his chosen career of small time con man.

For reasons no one understood and Ziggey never dwelled upon, people talked to him. Revealed things they told no one else. He had developed a knack for extracting information that many regretted revealing, if not the next day, a month or years later. He played the part of sympathetic and concerned listener to Oscar Award winning levels.

And so, on this his final night in the slammer, it was he who sought out Mr. Yoshi with his going away gift of the single malt Scotch. In the six months he'd been incarcerated, Ziggey had discovered all there was to know about Yoshi's background and why he was there, but instincts told him there was more to learn. Something that might be useful someday somewhere. If only to get the name of a relative or business associate that he might drop in the furtherance of some yet to be thought of scam.

"I still don't understand why a guy like you, wit your dough and connections, not to mention the lawyers you must have up the ying yang winds up in the joint? It just don't make no sense to me. Me, I understand. I get caught in a little harmless fun, make a few bucks and they nail me. And I ain't payin' no shyster to get me off. Rather do the six months and save the bread. But you...I just don't get it?" Ziggey said, leaning into Yoshi's ear then taking a long pull on his Coke and relaxing back in his chair.

Mr. Yoshi hunched forward almost sliding off his chair, took the bottle of Scotch and, spilling some, refilled his glass. Still leaning over the table he looked up at Ziggey and said, "I'm gonna tell ya, ole chap. It was merely a case of a misunderstanding and downright bigotry. No, bigotry was all it was. Your bloody government can't stand the thought of some poor yellow skinned immigrant making a decent living. It just galls them. So here I am because of some petty oversight. The Japanese example."

Of course Ziggey, as well as all the other inmates, knew that poor Mr. Yoshi's oversight was somewhere in the neighborhood of twenty five million dollars that those bigots in the IRS convicted him of not paying.

Taking a long swallow of his drink Mr. Yoshi continued, "By the way, my good man, oh, first let me again thank you for this most delightful of beverages, just why are you residing in this dingy place? Not some heinous crime against some poor devil I trust?"

"Naw, some people just ain't got no sense of humor. And like you, they made an example of me, not because I'm rich or nothin', but 'cause I'm just a hard working nobody. You really want to know, I'd be pleased to tell ya, but you gotta keep it to yourself. Nobody knows the whole truth. But you're a guy I know I can trust if you give me your word."

Tell a confidence, even if a lie, and get a confidence in return was a formula that had worked well for Ziggey since a kid in the school yard.

"My good fellow, you have both my word as a gentleman, and my undivided attention. Please go on with your story. I still have some friends - although that number has diminished considerably in these last few months - that might be of some help to you when you leave this tawdry place."

"Well, like I told ya." Ziggey, pleased with himself, went on. "I was made an example of. Things hadn't been going too well for me in my profession of choice. So one night I'm doin' my usual thing, sittin' at the bar at Jimmy's joint in the Village havin' a brew, bull shitin' with a coupla buddies waiting for lightning to strike. Well, this joint we go to, Jimmy's, gets a real mixed crowd. You know, a cross section of people, some not so classy and some real classy rich types."

People like the Village' think it's colorful, like to look at the freaks and then go home. Also get some pretty famous

3

actors, what comes in. Lots of 'em started out in the Village and like to come back an' show off. And there's this acting school in the neighborhood, kids who think after twenty classes at five bucks a crack they're gonna be stars."

"That's all very interesting Mr. Zignorelli, but please get to the point. Just why are you here?"

"Sorry pal, once I get started talkin'...anyway I get this job as an extra in a movie they're shootin' in the Village. Another one of them stupid mob movies. Guy comes to me at Jimmy's one night sez he's some assistant director and I'd be perfect for this flick. No lines or anything, but you get meals and $42.50 a day cash five days work. Chump change to a guy like you, but what the hell, two hundred and change plus a week of free food. I ain't doin nothin' else and you never know what opportunities come up. So now I'm in show biz. Never met so many assholes in my life. I just couldn't resist. We got maybe a hundred extras in this thing all thinkin' they're gonna be discovered. So I discover them. For a small fee of course. Everyday I get there early, and I hang around the director makin' like I'm his best buddy. He's so busy he don't notice. I walk away sayin' things, like "great, see ya at dinner tonight." I know I'm bein' watched. Doesn't take a minute before some of them starts shinin' up to me. "Who are you?" "You're a friend of the directors?" "Maybe you could introduce me?" "I got a lot of theater experience." Crap like that."

"So, being the helpful guy that I am, I spread the word that for a small cash fee, not the ten percent agents get, I can get them plenty of work. I know people. These schmucks are so desperate and stupid not only do they buy it, but they tell their friends."

"You never told them you were an agent. Just that you would help them for less money then agents charge. I don't see anything criminal about that. Maybe a tad less than moral. People get what they deserve I always say." Mr. Yoshi responded sympathetically.

"Yeah, well, that's not how the Union saw it. How was I to know most of those putzes were union members of the Screen Actors Guild. The last day of shooting, a union rep' is working as an extra, and he ain't buying my shit. Blows the fucking whistle all the way to Hollywood and they fry my ass. Make an example of me. Haul my ass into court, grand larceny! Can you believe that? Called me a celebrity cause."

"Cause celeb." Mr. Yoshi said. "It's a French expression meaning..."

"Whatever, like I said, they nailed me. Front page news in all the show biz papers. Anyway, I'm outta here tomorrow. Ain't been too bad, six months and I got to meet some nice guys like you. Who knows maybe someday we'll meet again. I gotta go pack. It was nice meetin' ya." Ziggey said shaking Mr. Yoshi's hand.

Mr. Yoshi got up to leave with Ziggey, still maintaining the handshake with one hand and picking up the bottle of Scotch with the other and taking a not very gentlemanly swig from the bottle. Swaying down the corridor to their rooms Mr. Yoshi put his arm around Ziggey's shoulder with some affection, but more for stability. Stopping outside his room he insisted Ziggey come in for a nightcap. Ziggey started to decline, when he remembered that he hadn't gotten what he came after having been so engrossed in his own story.

"That's real nice of ya, Mr. Yoshi, but it's close to lights out and I gotta pack." He said while allowing himself to be pulled into the room.

"Actually, I could use a drink, I'm startin' to get a little nervous. Something could go wrong tomorrow and they don't let me out on some technical thing. Ya never know. Happened to me once before..." Then he caught himself. Let the man talk. "So Mr. Yoshi, I heard all the rumors, but what really happened? I still don't get why a guy like you gets nailed. You gotta have people in the right places."

"That was exactly my problem. My bloody people! Scared little wimps. After all I did for them the bloody bastards turned on me. I made them more money in a few years then they ever had a hope of amassing in a life time. And the fools turned on me. Slightest hint of trouble and they couldn't wait to turn states evidence to cover their puny little asses. It's appalling, absolutely appalling."

He stopped what was becoming an angry tirade to pour himself another drink and Ziggey thought he detected tears welling up in Yoshi's eyes. So he decided to try some compassion.

"I know what you mean. Been there myself. Can't trust nobody no more. Couldn't you threaten them? You musta had somethin' you could hold over them? Some hook you coulda reeled in?"

Appreciating Ziggey's concern and having regained his composure Yoshi sat down and continued.

"Not quite that simple my friend. Actually when one deals in those numbers it's not uncommon for ...How shall I explain? Well as you Americans like to say, not everything was always kosher. Sometimes things have to move more expeditiously than either prudence or the law would dictate. I'm sure a man of your experience understands?"

"Sure. Sometimes you just gotta go with your gut backed up with cash. Screw the rules."

Ziggey was psyched now. He felt an offer coming. Or at least some favor he might be able to do for Yoshi. Something he'd be well rewarded for. He knew, in spite of the huge fines Yoshi paid that guys like him had plenty stashed away. He decided to push before this guy passed out from the booze.

"I don't mean to be pushy or nothin', but is there somethin' I could maybe do for you on the outside? I got lots of connections. Don't let my current situation fool you. This is only a temporary set back." Ziggey said hopefully.

Yoshi, pensively, hesitated looking at the floor making Ziggey nervous. Was he going to offer him something of value, or throw up? Was this fifty dollar bottle of Scotch going to pay off or not?

Pulling himself up, looking Ziggey square in the eye he said, "My good man I've come to a decision. I'm not sure why exactly, but I feel you're a man I can trust."

"Here it comes," Ziggey said mostly to himself.

"Did you say something?" Yoshi asked.

"No sir, just that you definitely can trust me."

"OK. Then sit down and listen." Yoshi said who was now all business and gave the appearance of never having had a drink in his life, let alone almost a bottle this evening. He then went to a small night table next to his bed and took out a floppy computer disk.

"I assume you know what this is and know how to extract the information contained?"

Ziggey knew what it was, but hadn't the slightest notion of how to extract anything from this piece of plastic. Now was not the time to be stupid. He'd extract whatever Yoshi wanted him to extract when the time came. He just kept his mouth shut, nodding affirmatively.

"On this you will find the names and addresses of some very rich people. Not celebrities nor people you hear about on the evening news. Some of these were associates of mine and others friends of theirs whom I socialized with in the past. People who pandered to me, or to put it more crudely tried to kiss my ass every waking moment. In their fever to curry favor with me, they talked too much. Told me things they never should have told anyone. Foolishly took me into their confidence in the hopes that I might betray something of value to them. It's an old con game. Give a confidence and hope for the same in return." He said winking at Ziggey.

Shit! Ziggey thought. He had never seen such a transformation in a man before. Ten minutes earlier he thought the guy was going to pass out. Now he thought he was being addressed by the Chairman of the Board of some big company. Had this guy been testing him all evening?

"You seem distracted Mr. Zignorelli." Yoshi said with a slight smile. "Shall I go on? Or might we discuss this upon my release some months from now?"

"Uh, No. No sir. Please go on. I'm just a little jumpy about tomorrow that's all. Didn't mean no disrespect or nothin'." He replied, nervously hoping that Yoshi would in fact go on. That he hadn't blown it.

"Fine then. In addition to names and addresses you will find a dossier about each of these people including such things as location of alarm systems, safes, how many servants, whether they have pets, and other pertinent information. I should also make it clear to you at this time that I wasn't to the Manor Born. My background is not that dissimilar to yours although I've had a tad more fortune with my skills than you have. My language, clothing, and social skills have been carefully acquired and cultivated." Sensing that Ziggey was about to interrupt, Yoshi held up his hand.

"Let me go on. I want you to know whom you are dealing with. I too was brought up in the streets. Not in New York's tame Greenwich Village, but in what has come to be known as South Central, Los Angeles. Unlike you, from the time I was able to hold one, I carried a gun. We were not exactly welcomed to the neighborhood. My parents' shack -- I can't even dignify it as a house -- was repeatedly torched and vandalized. But enough of that. I just want to assure you that beneath this manicured exterior, lies a man tenfold you and your friends."

Ziggey, not easily shocked, almost wet his pants. Just when you thought you could figure anybody, you get nailed. He felt like a schmuck. Nothing worse then a con getting caught at his own game. But wait a minute, he thought, maybe we're gonna be partners? This could be good? Finally got someone behind me with some real bread.

"The town that these folks live in is East Hampton." Yoshi continued. "It's one of several, largely, affluent towns on the Eastern end of Long Island collectively called the Hamptons. I'm sure you've heard of them so you would know that it is a vacation resort as well. Much of the time some of the homes are vacant. Not all, I would caution you. More and more people are living there year round now, but that's for you to research. Now to the point. Along with a fragmented list of such things as coin and stamp collections, some extremely valuable, one of those homes has millions of dollars in stolen paintings. Masterpieces that have disappeared from museums and private collections since World War II. There exists an underground market for these treasures. But once owned, most never surface unless due to some calamity of nature. Or some stupid relative inheriting them. I want some of those paintings! I want to hurt that bastard. He's so smug. I want to get back at all of them. It was with the money I made them, and the people they met through me, that they were able to acquire such wealth. The guy with the paintings in particular. They're rightfully mine and I want them to do with as I please."

You could have driven an eighteen-wheeler through Ziggey's mouth. He never contemplated anything on such a grand scale. This was big time. The stuff you see in the movies. He was speechless for the first time in his life. But the carrot was there. A twenty four caret, gold carrot. One more deal and off to South America for life, he thought.

"You seem a little apprehensive?" Yoshi said interrupting Ziggey's thoughts. "You're thinking this is over your head. Too big for you and your friends. Let me dispel what I suspect is your main fear: what happens to you if you're caught with million dollar paintings? I'll do life. Not so. You simply say you found them and were planning to turn them over to the authorities. No one for a moment would anyone assume that you were either the original thief nor knew where the paintings were. You were hanging out in an old loft looking through junk and you simply found

9

them. You have stolen, stolen art. The bastard that you took them from can't open his mouth. He can't come forward to press charges. If he did he would immediately be arrested and questioned as to how he attained the paintings."

Ziggey was buying this. This was true. You steal something that's been stolen the original stealer can't admit it.

"And to sweeten the pot," Yoshi continued, "You get to keep whatever else you find, as in the aforementioned coin and stamp collections, along with hundreds of thousands of dollars worth of furs and jewels all readily fenceable. Not to mention cash that I'm sure the IRS has never heard about."

A con man's dream come true.

CHAPTER TWO

It was a perfect early fall day in New England as the train rolled past the kind of towns that inspired Christmas cards. The fall foliage was at its peak, the colors so startling that audible oohs and aahs could be heard from some of the passengers. But not Ziggey. He seemed in a trance as he sat on his freedom ride home fingering the three and half inch floppy that could be his "fuck you" money.

Mr. Yoshi's proposal was way beyond anything he had ever done or contemplated doing in the past. He was after all just a simple scam artist of little repute, not a house burglar, and certainly not several houses.

But life presents few golden opportunities and Yoshi's proposal certainly was golden. He had to come up with a plan. And strategic planning was not his long suit. He was a guy whose idea of planning ahead was what he might do the coming weekend if it was already Friday.

Friends had wanted to meet him at the prison on his release and drive to the nearest bar to celebrate, but he refused the offer. He needed to be alone to think. He wasn't even going straight home. There would be friends and neighbors on the street who would want to celebrate. He wouldn't even go to Jimmy's till later that night. Instead he decided to go someplace where no one would recognize him or think to look for him. The Metropolitan Museum of Art on Fifth Avenue.

But first, before a plan could be devised, he had a bigger problem. He hadn't the foggiest notion what one did with a floppy disk, other then it had something to do with computers. Who could he trust that owned a computer? Somebody at Jimmy's? Besides the actors, a lot of college kids from NYU hung out there. The burgers, chili, pizza and pitchers of beer were cheap. Maybe if he gave some kid a few bucks, he would print out a copy? No, that was risky, actually stupid. The kid would obviously read it. Maybe if he stood there and took the paper from the printer himself? He had no idea if it was one page or twenty. The kid would care less and never see the printed page. Wait a minute, he thought, did what you print show up on the screen as you printed? He didn't know. But he sure wasn't going to let anyone read this stuff. Something else he'd have to research before making the offer. Maybe he could blindfold the kid, tell him it was something personal. His will maybe? Lying was his long suit, and besides this wasn't a lie. Not that it mattered.

He caught himself. He was over thinking step one. That was the least of his problems. Start thinking about a plan, he chastised himself. You got a lot bigger fish to fry, schmuck!

The train pulled into Grand Central, and the day being what it was, he decided to walk to the Museum approximately two miles away. This would be the longest walk he'd been able to take in one direction in the last six months. Walking helped him think.

He walked up Madison Avenue for awhile then on a whim turned west on Forty Ninth Street heading to Fifth Avenue. When he turned the corner it was deja vu. The entire block from Madison to Fifth was closed to traffic. Both sides of the street were lined with a film company's equipment trucks and Winnebagos that served as actors dressing rooms. He remembered it well. Ziggey thought about avoiding the block in case some of the crew from his old movie was there and still bitter. Screw 'em. He'd served his time. And maybe someone famous was there. Con men are starstruck also.

Fortunately, no one recognized him. Turning uptown on Fifth he was amazed. The Avenue was closed to traffic from Forty Ninth to Fiftieth Street in front of Saks Fifth Avenue. There were two huge Cherry Pickers in the middle of the street raised up three or four stories. One had lights, the other the camera. They were shooting through one of Saks' upper windows.

Stopping to gaze, he said out loud, "Jeeze! The power these movie bastards have. Probably could close the whole damn city if they wanted?"

"What'd you say?" A guy next to him asked.

"I said, it's nuts what these Hollywood fucks can get away with. Like we ain't got enough trouble gettin' around."

"Yeah, I suppose you're right." The guy answered, "I even heard they could hire cops and not just the off-duty ones."

"Damn, that's power for ya!" Ziggey shouted as the group he'd been standing with happily parted to let him through.

When he got to Central Park South he decided it would be nice to walk through Central Park. Besides he was getting tired and hungry. He'd get a Sabretts hot dog with sauerkraut and mustard and sit and relax a while. Maybe the more bucolic setting would help him think.

And it did! Like a shot. Just as his bottom touched the park bench, he jumped up yelling, "I got it! That's it! Jesus, fucking Christ! That's it! That's the god damn plan!"

This outburst quickly cleared the area of everyone within earshot except a well-coifed old lady and a middle aged homeless black man who rushed over to Ziggey with his hands raised waving, yelling, "Hallelujah! brother. Hallelujah! You found the Lord!"

As he attempted to embrace Ziggey, Ziggey backed away tripping over the blue-haired lady's thousand dollar runt of a dog.

"What're you, some fuckin' nut? Get away from me."
Ziggey said addressing the black man.

To which the indignant lady replied, "Get away from
you? I want your name and address young man. If you've
hurt my Ginger, you'll pay. And pay dearly. My husband is
one of the biggest attorneys in New York."

"Lady, go to hell."

"Well, I never..." she stammered while reaching for him.
Ziggey brushed her aside and added, "Outta my way lady, I
got a movie to produce."

As he strutted away, very pleased with himself, the
black man yelled, "May the Lord be with you my brother."

It'd be about fuckin' time, he thought.

CHAPTER THREE

The size of the crowd at Jimmy's that evening was unexpected for a week night and not particularly appreciated by Ziggey. He had neither the time nor the inclination to celebrate. He was a man on a mission. He had plans to make, complicated plans.

He was going to need help. This was by no means a solo operation. Something he didn't like. Ziggey always worked alone. No one to rat you out. No one to worry about. The times he was caught, it was his own fault. Had no one to blame but himself. And this was not going to be a fly by the seat of your pants operation. He wasn't going to be able to wing it as he had in the past. A smart mouth and street smarts had always served him well. But what he was thinking now was big time. But maybe the guy in the park was right, maybe God would be on his side with this one. After all, he thought while smiling and shaking hands, I ain't a bad guy. He thought like most con artists. I never hurt no one. Just took some money from some fools that deserved to be taken.

Ziggey figured that the regular crowd would be there. That Jimmy would buy him a steak diner, and drinks would be on the house. Meantime, he feigned excitement with the over-enthusiastic response of some of the regulars. Shit, he hadn't exactly done hard time he thought to himself. The last six months was more like a vacation.

"Good to see you again, Greg. How's the wife?"

"Hey Sal! Missed ya babe."

And so it went for a half hour, until Ziggey was finally seated in a back corner booth facing so he could see all and all could see him.

There were no women in Ziggey's life at this time. Matter of fact there had been damn few over the last ten years. Broads had never been high on Ziggey's "Who Do You Trust Most" List. There were some one-nighters which, more often than not, were one hour. Ziggey's idea of foreplay was turning down the covers. He didn't like sharing his apartment. Didn't want to worry what sort of incriminating evidence might be lying around. Broads were snoopy. Always asking questions and looking around, mostly to see if there was evidence of any other broads having been there recently.

Besides he'd been married once a long time ago and the bitch left him 'cause he never had a straight job. Or so she said. If she wanted some nine-to-five putz it was fine with him.

Jimmy arrived, saying as he sat down, "So, Ziggey, you alright? You need anything? A few bucks, a new apartment, a job? You know I could throw you a coupla bar shifts if it would help?"

"Thanks Jimmy, but I'm cool. Everything's OK. If I wasn't, you know I'd come to you first. Howyoudoin'? Business been OK?"

"I'm fine. Same ole shit, payin' my bills and tryin' to put a few bucks away. I'm makin' a livin'. That's better then most can say."

"Where's Richie? I ain't seen him. He still coming in?" Ziggey asked.

"Yeah, sure. Should be in soon, he's teachin' a class tonight." Jimmy responded.

"What about Bobby? He gettin' any work or still chasing after that TV pot of gold?"

Ziggey's inquiry about those two was asked with more then casual interest. He had an ulterior motive.

16

"Bobby's still chasin'." Jimmy answered. "Gets an audition for a commercial every once in a while. Keeps him goin'. Who knows, maybe he'll hit someday. You gotta have luck."

Richard "Richie" Kennedy and Robert "Bobby" Bernstein were regulars at Jimmy's, and drinking friends of Ziggey's.

Robert Bernstein, is a frustrated, middle aged, writer-actor. As a younger man he had held several middle management film and TV production jobs. Several years ago, through a friend, he had the opportunity to move from behind the camera to the front. He played a small continuing role on a prime time television series that hooked him forever. In addition he had done several commercials. Since then, while pursuing the acting dream, he has taken to writing screenplays, and one novel for which he has received enough kudos, albeit no contracts, to keep that pursuit alive.

Richard, on the other hand, is man who had found his dream. A retired college professor, somewhere in his late fifties or early sixties, no one knew or cared, he was now a full time acting teacher, and sometime actor. He taught at a well known acting school around the corner from Jimmy's. All his life Richard had acted in college productions, little theater groups, and ultimately some off Broadway productions. Now having gained great character actor looks he was occasionally getting small parts in feature films.

CHAPTER FOUR

"Hey, how are ya? Didn't know you were getting out so soon. It's good to see you. Jimmy, why didn't you tell me he was getting out?" Robert said all in one breath as he approached Ziggey's table, hand extended.

"I didn't know myself. Listen guys, have fun. Everything's with me tonight. I gotta get back to work. Check on the kitchen." Jimmy said excusing himself.

Robert vigorously shook Ziggeys' hand, sat down and ordered a Dewars and water.

"So, howyadoin, Bobby?" Ziggey asked. "Got anything cookin'?"

"Nope. Not a damn thing. Got another agent so now I'm ignored by two of 'em."

"How about that book you wrote a while ago?" Ziggey asked with what would pass for sincere concern.

"Not a damn thing. Got tired of rejection notices so stopped sending it out." Robert said with resignation.

"What're you doin' for bread?"

"You know, same old shit. I help out here some nights, get some construction from work from time to time, do some apartment painting..."

Ziggey interrupting. "You're lucky you got all them skills, me, I only got one trade, but listen, I got an idea I'm workin' on, might be something in it for you if you're interested?" Ziggey said in a hushed voice.

"You know me Ziggey, if I can make a buck, and still have time for an audition, I'm interested." Robert answered excitedly.

"Not something I wanna talk about here."

"Wait a minute. I forgot who I was talking to." Robert asked deflated. "This is legitimate isn't it? I mean what with your recent holiday upstate an all, you're not thinking about...?"

Ziggey interrupted him.

"You got nothin' to worry about. I got some kinks to work out yet. But what I got in mind for you is strictly on the up and up. Not to worry."

At this point they were joined by Richard who, uncharacteristically quiet, slid into the booth next to Robert.

"Richie, howyadoin? Jeeze, don't answer. You look like shit. Worse than me." Ziggey observed.

"You ain't been in the can or something? What's the matter, man?"

"Nothing. Just a little tired." Richard lied.

"Bullshit!" Ziggey said. "Don't give me that crap. This is your friend Ziggey you're talkin' to. You look like twenty miles of bad road. What the fuck happened, man? Someone die or something?"

"I don't want to talk about it now." Richard said as the waitress asked for his order.

"I'll have a Vodka and tonic...Wait a minute, make it a double, easy on the tonic."

"You ok, Richard?" the waitress asked doing a double take as she started to leave. "You're not sick or anything? You don't look so good."

"I'm fine, honey. Just a little hung over. Thanks for asking though." He responded, turning back to Ziggey, forcing himself to act cheerful. "So, Mr. Z, how'd it go? Make lots of license plates?"

19

"Naw it wasn't that kinda joint." Ziggey answered taking the question literally. "I worked in the canteen. Cashier. Shows you how smart they are. Guess they figured I wouldn't steal nothin' from other cons. Boy, were they wrong. Piece a cake. You know we had a lot a rich guys there. Never spent a minute on the street. I could make a good livin' in a joint like that, but I ain't too fond of the sleeping arrangements. You know me, I'm a night person and they don't let you walk around after nine when I'm used to just goin' out."

Richard and Robert had always gotten a big kick out of Ziggey's slant on life. Nothing ever seemed to bother him. Situations that would have sent both of them into years of therapy, he sluffed off with a joke. That was part of the cement that bound these three unlikely types together. It was a friendship not uncommon in New York. Disparate types didn't shy away from each other, but usually found some common ground. Frequently it was sports, but sometimes, when you scratched the surface, you discovered a more profound bond.

In spite of Ziggeys' chosen profession, he was a decent, caring guy. So they thought. His life of crime was an addiction that he wouldn't shake. He never held a straight job for more than two weeks. He couldn't. They always ended in his scamming his boss or other employees.

Robert liked him for his streetwise advice. A perspective he never got from his more educated friends. Richard just liked him because he was colorful. To Richard this was a guy from a yet unpublished play. A latter day Damon Runyon character. Ziggey was ongoing theater.

Both Ziggey and Robert knew full well that something serious was troubling Richard, and both knew not to press the issue. Somewhere between the third and fifth Vodkas, it would come out.

And so it did, as silently predicted.

"Listen guys," Richard said leaning into the table in a hushed tone as the waitress left his fourth drink on the table. "I gotta talk to someone, but you gotta promise me you'll keep it to yourselves. I don't even want Jimmy to know.

Man, this was scary, both Ziggey and Robert thought. They had never seen the here-to-fore happy-go-lucky Richard like this. A menu of horrible thoughts crossed both their minds starting with cancer and ending with cirrhosis of the liver.

Ziggey started to say something, but Richard put his hand up stopping him.

"Don't interrupt or I'll never get through this." Richard intoned. "It's simple, I'm ruined. Life as I've known it is over. Everything is gone. The bastards have taken everything away from me. If I hadn't bumped into Benny outside who told me you were here I wouldn't have come in. Matter of fact been thinking of not going anywhere ever again. Bailing out."

Ziggey could hold back no longer. "Hey man, don't talk that shit. Ain't nothin' that fuckin' bad it can't be worked out. I don't want to ever hear that shit from you again. The Z man can work anything out!"

"Not this one I'm afraid." Richard continued. "You know I took early retirement. Hell, I was only fifty-five. I really wasn't ready for the rocking chair, but the bastards made it sound so good.

"I played the game for twenty five years, towed the line, never made a ripple. Give it to good ole Richard. He'll do it. And like a schmuck I did."

Both Ziggey and Robert breathed an audible sigh of relief. Whatever was troubling their friend wasn't terminal. It had something to do with the university.

"To put it simply and crudely, gentlemen, they screwed me good! Took away my pension."

"How could they do that?" Ziggey interrupted, incredulous.

"They can't." Robert added. "That money is guaranteed by the government. It's a city owned university. There's got to be some mistake, Richard. You sure of your facts on this?"

"Oh, I'm sure all right. Got it right here in black and white." He said while reaching into his inside jacket pocket to produce documentation.

"Let me see that." Robert said taking the papers and quickly scanning the first page. "What the hell are you talkin about? For a Ph.D., you can sure be dumb sometimes, Doctor! They're not taking it away, just putting it off till you're sixty three. What's the big deal? I don't know how old you are, but it can't be too far away."

"I'll tell you what the big deal is." Richard continued, exasperated by this lack of understanding. "I'm just fifty nine. That's four years to go. I got a package when I left four years ago that included a nice check. Money's gone. You know I live pretty well. The pension was supposed to kick in next year on my sixtieth birthday. I'm screwed. Who the hell do you think is going to hire a sixty year old guy? I'll tell you. Nobody!"

"You still got that job around the corner? Don't you?" Ziggey asked.

"That doesn't cover my bar tab."

"What about acting?" Robert asked. "You've had some good parts the last coupla years."

"Not enough. Not nearly enough. I don't know what the hell I'm gonna do." Richard said while motioning to the waitress to bring another round for the table.

"Shit man, I thought you had the big "C" or somethin'." Ziggey said, putting his arm on Richard's shoulder. "Not to worry my friend. The Z man is here with a solution. Strictly legit. Tomorrow we get together, the three of us, in my apartment, and I'll lay out the plan. Bobby's already in."

CHAPTER FIVE

Ziggey had, what everybody that wasn't a landlord considered, the ultimate New York City apartment. Rent controlled. He lived on one of the most charming tree-lined streets in the West Village. A neighborhood that had changed in the last forty years from working class trades people and yet-to-be-discovered artists, writers, and actors, to the far more affluent.

Through no particular wisdom or foresight, Ziggey had done the smartest thing in his life. When his grandfather died leaving his grandmother alone, Ziggey moved in with her and had his name added to the lease.

She needed help and he needed to get out of his parents' house in Brooklyn. The berating of his father to get a regular job and the fights between his mother and father made the decision easy.

So Ziggey still lived in this four room apartment paying a paltry one hundred twenty four dollars and sixty three cents a month rent. The other floors in his Brownstone had been converted to one and two bedroom apartments that rented from twenty four hundred to four thousand a month. And there was a waiting list for those. Even a minor score would pay his rent for years.

The meeting with Richie and Bobby had to be held in private, therefore in his apartment, even though Richard and Robert thought this odd. They had never been invited to Ziggey's before and were wary.

Ziggey wasn't approaching this with the arrogance of a know it all. Unlike stupid people, Ziggey knew what he didn't know. And Ziggey wasn't stupid. Had circumstances been different at home, Ziggey might have graduated cum laude from some university. He knew he couldn't pull this off without the aid of others.

Neither Robert nor Richard were knocking 'em dead in their chosen professions. Bobby was getting more bitter and cynical as the months passed with less and less hope for stardom, let alone a regular gig.

And Richie was one angry ex-professor. The system that he had supported so fervently all of his life, had betrayed him. It turned out that there was a clause in Richard's early retirement package that stated if the University's investments were less profitable than projected, early retirement plans would revert to normal retirement age.

So Ziggey felt sure he would have the help he needed from these two.

Literally crawling out of bed at noon, Richard, had forgotten about Ziggey's offer of the night before. It wasn't something he had taken seriously at the time anyway. He figured Ziggey was just running off at the mouth in an attempt to make him feel better. After all, what the hell could Ziggey do for him?

When the phone rang Richard made sure his answering machine was on. He would monitor any calls unless it was the university admitting some mistake.

It was Robert reminding him of this evening's meeting with Ziggey, and asking if he would like to meet him for a burger before the meeting.

The mere suggestion of food turned Richard's stomach. But the reminder of tonight's meeting buoyed his spirits a little. He now remembered dismissing the offer last night as just so much talk. But what the hell, it couldn't hurt to listen, he thought. Maybe he met someone in that country club prison that took a liking to him? Maybe, he went on optimistically, someone was returning a favor? And he had said that Robert was already in so it must be OK. Robert was straight as a stick. He had done a lot of things in his life, but never anything, as far as he knew, illegal. He would call Robert back when he felt a little better and meet him for diner to see if he could shed some light on Ziggey's plan.

Richard met Robert at Jimmy's at five-thirty for soup and a sandwich. Unfortunately, Robert could not offer any insight into Ziggey's offer, but he too was suspicious. Granted, they both knew that not everybody Ziggey hung around with was a felon. After all, weren't they friendly with him? And there were others, so maybe this would be Kosher?

Robert stopped at a local deli on the way to their meeting picking up a six pack of beer assuming that Ziggey would not be a gracious host.

They were both surprised when Ziggey led them into the kitchen and they saw his kitchen table strewn with books, manuals and legal pads. This was not a guy who wrote or read books.

"Gentlemen. Welcome to my humble, rent-controlled pad." Ziggey loved the ring of the words rent-controlled particularly when in the company of someone paying four times the rent with half the square footage.

"Yeah, Yeah. Ziggey we know it's rent-controlled." they said in unison.

"So what's this offer you have for us that I've apparently already agreed to." Robert said while opening a beer and offering one to Richard. Ziggey didn't drink beer. Cheap wine and sometimes, if someone was buying, Scotch.

"Sit down. Take a load off. I'll tell ya. I'm still working out some of the details, but that's where you guys come in. I seek your knowledge and council. And for this I am prepared to pay." Ziggey said clearing the table as he spoke.

Richard in the meantime had been looking at the book titles while Robert was putting the remaining beers in the fridge. "Making a Movie with a Small Budget," "Movie Making for the Beginner," and assorted manuals on equipment, shooting on location, and a dictionary of film making terms.

"What's all this?" Richard asked incredulously. "You're not thinking about making a movie, are you?"

"Not thinking. Doing!" Ziggey replied.

"You gotta be kidding!" Robert said joining the table and fingering the books. "What do you know about making a movie?"

"Not much. Well a little. You forget so fast. It was my movie experience that landed me in the slammer. So, I ain't completely without knowledge on the subject. Besides, that's what I need you guys for."

Richard and Robert looked at each other and smiled.

"So what's the deal?" Robert asked taking a long swallow of beer. "Wait. Let me guess. You met some millionaire stock broker in the slammer who was framed and he's got a great story to tell. You're gonna do a documentary, sell it to HBO, the guy gets sprung, pays you a million dollars. His twenty-one year old virgin daughter from Greenwich, I mean Greenwich, Connecticut, marries you out of gratitude and you live happily ever after on her trust fund. How'm I doin', so far?"

Richard's face was contorted with laughter. He loved Robert's ability to come up with an outrageous story at a moments notice. If only he would write as he spoke, he often told him.

Ziggey was not as amused. However he couldn't suppress a smile. He too liked Bobby's penchant for story telling.

"Not a bad idea, Bobby." Ziggey said with a chuckle, then turning serious. "But there ain't no virgins in Connecticut. Now if you guys is finished with your fuckin' around, I'd like to get down to business.

CHAPTER SIX

In deference to their friend and his apparent seriousness, Robert and Richard fell silent.

"Go ahead, Ziggey, I'm sorry, I couldn't resist." Robert said, getting another beer and sitting at the table.

"Yes, go ahead." Richard said. "If it's got anything to do with movies, I'm interested."

"OK." Ziggey said taking a deep breath. "Here's the deal." Ziggey was about to tell the biggest and most profitable or most costly lie of his life.

"This is the new Mr. 'Z' talking. Mr. 'Z' the producer. I know I ain't never done nothing like this before, but a guy I know is given me a shot at it. If we can pull this off we can all make some real dough.

"Here's the deal. I did a few favors for this guy in the slammer. A rich guy. Anyway we got to talkin', about friends and associates and stuff like that. I told him about you guys. Wanted him to know that not all of my friends was scuzz balls. Anyway, he comes up with this idea for me to make a low budget movie for him. Guys got connections all over the world, especially in Asian countries, and he says he can sell any American movie for big bucks there."

Robert interrupted, now both serious and interested. "That's true, Ziggey, I just read an article in Variety last week about how they go for American flicks in Hong Kong, Singapore, all over the Orient. Doesn't matter how crappy they are either. Long as it's got American actors. They've

27

been watching so much of our old stuff for years that they gobble up anything new."

Ziggey, continuing the lie. "Yeah, that's exactly what my friend told me. Anyhow, he said if we can make one half way decent movie, he could sell as many as we make after that."

"What kind of movie does it have to be?" Richard asked, his interest peaked. "I mean if you're thinking action adventure or something like that, it isn't cheap. You need special effects and a big crew and that costs a lot. Just what kind of budget are we talking about?"

"Well, I'm not exactly sure." Ziggey said slowly while thinking of an answer since he had no idea what it cost to make a movie of any size. "You guys know more about that stuff than me. I've been doing a little research here in these books and it don't seem that expensive unless you have big stars and that ain't necessary. I figure we could probably do something my friend could sell, for maybe a quarter of a mill? How's that sound?"

"That's not a lot of money to do a feature film Ziggey." Robert said. "I mean for that kind of bread it can't be a union shoot, but if we watch the pennies we could put together something. Depends on the story, can't be anything where you have to build fancy sets."

"Yeah, that's what I thought." Ziggey said encouraged by this serious response.

"Just what is the story? You got a script we could read?" Richard asked.

More trouble for Ziggey. He should have figured these guys would asks lots of questions, none of which he could answer. Usually he could talk his way out of or around any obstacle. This was different. These guys were educated.

"Not exactly. Not yet anyway." Ziggey answered fumbling. "I figured you guys could come up with something. What about all that stuff you been writing Bobby? You gotta have something we could use. Even if it

28

ain't finished yet, you know we could sorta wing it. You're a smart guy shouldn't be hard for you. Besides, this don't have to be no great thing." Ziggey's mind was racing as he searched for logical reasons to keep these two interested. "My friend told me as long as you got some actors that they can recognize, the movie don't have to be any great shakes."

Richard was skeptical, but Robert was getting more and more fired up. This could be a break through, he thought, providing the movie has any credibility. At the very least he would have his long sought after screen credit and maybe a small part in the movie. What did he have to lose?

The backer of this project, Mr. Yoshi, had no idea of Ziggeys' plan. Ziggey was taking a gamble that Yoshi would back him. Yoshi had simply charged Ziggey with the task of coming up with a plan that would enable him to steal the stolen art he coveted. He didn't care how this was accomplished and didn't want to know. All he said was, "What ever you need, you got it, but don't call or write to me. We are not to speak again. Whatever you need, you contact my wife."

So Ziggey figured the cost was in bounds. Besides, what the hell was a lousy two hundred fifty thou' to a guy who screwed the government out of twenty five million? Sure he paid a hell of a fine, but there were frequent stories about the lavish life style still maintained by Mrs. Yoshi and the kids. Only difference was the children were transferred from fancy American private schools to fancy British ones. Big deal. She still had the mansion in South Hampton, the ten room duplex at the Beresford on Central Park West, a house in the South of France, an apartment in Paris, and a condo in L. A. This was not a family about to be rendered homeless.

Ziggey had been given a secure phone number to contact Mrs. Yoshi. Even though his attorneys assured Yoshi that the FBI and SEC wire taps had been removed after his conviction, he remained paranoid. All the phones, faxes, and computer modems were swept weekly by his security people.

Should Ziggey need anything, they could arrange to meet, by accident, in some public place. Why would this ex-con be visiting the home of a woman such as Mrs. Yoshi.

So Ziggey rightly felt that he had the full financial support of Yoshi. Money would not be the problem. Credibility was the only issue. Could he convince an entire community that this was a real movie company shooting a real movie? The presence of recognizable actors would be key to pulling this scam off. He would also need to have Richard and Robert enthusiastically promoting the project. He would stay in the background as much as possible. Ziggey knew his limitations.

CHAPTER SEVEN

The next two weeks passed quickly for a very busy Ziggey. To his great satisfaction, Robert had jumped into this project with an energy Ziggey had never seen in him. Robert was sold and loving it.

Ziggey found it easy to agree with every suggestion Robert made, particularly since he had no idea what Robert was talking about and didn't care as long as this was going to look like a real movie company.

When Robert asked if he could be the Line Producer as well as writer, Ziggey complied after it was explained to him what Line Producer duties were.

Robert would take care of the pesky, but all important details, such as camera, audio, and lighting rentals as soon as he completed a rough draft of his script. He would present Ziggey with a budget estimate that Ziggey might send to his mysterious backer for approval.

Robert also recommended that, as well as acting in the film, Richard be the Director in the interests of cutting costs.

All fine with Ziggey. He had far bigger issues to deal with. First, he had to find someone to print out the information on that three-and-a-half inch plastic disc. Robert had a computer and certainly could do it, but that wouldn't do. Robert would undoubtedly read the information. He had to find out if when you run something through a printer it has to show up on the screen. If not, then he could find someone at Jimmy's who would do him a favor. One of the kid waiters must have a computer, he thought.

Problem number one solved. Ziggey was approached by David, a new waiter and NYU film student when he stopped in one afternoon for coffee.

"I understand, Mr. Zignorelli, that you're a film maker." he said serving him coffee at the bar.

"Uh, yeah kid." Ziggey had to remember from time to time what he was now. Gossip was the main course at Jimmy's if it had anything to do with show business. Everyone was looking for a connection. As in most Village restaurants and bars, all the waiters and bartenders were biding time till they got that show biz break.

"Me too." David said to a distracted and disinterested Ziggey. "I mean not like you. Not yet anyway. I'm still at NYU film school. You probably know some of my professors you being in the business and all? I don't mean to be pushy or anything, but I only have one semester to go and I have plenty of spare time so if there's anything I can do for you or your company I'd love the chance to get some work. You know, a professional credit. Production Assistant, messenger, anything would be great."

"You got a computer kid?" Ziggey asked matter of factually.

"Yeah, yes sir! I sure do! State of the Art. Just upgraded my hard drive, and added 32 megs of RAM and..."

"OK, OK, spare me the details." Ziggey interrupted. "I may have a little project for you. I ain't too familiar with computers, but I need to have a little something printed from this thing." Ziggey said as he produced the disc from his shirt pocket.

"No problem sir. Piece of cake. Let me have it and I'll do it tonight and bring it back to you tomorrow."

"Hold on. This doesn't leave my hands. It's very confidential stuff. Let me ask you a question. Say I let you help me with this thing? When you do whatever it is you have to do, does what's on this have to show up on the screen?"

"No, of course not. Not if you don't want it to. I can make the screen blank. You see..."

"Don't explain. I ain't interested in technical stuff. So I can just take the paper from the printer. Right?"

"Yes sir. You can come over to my apartment and take each page from the printer yourself. I got a HP Laser that makes letter quality..."

"Yeah, fine. When're you off? I gotta get this done right away."

"Five. May I ask what is on the disc?"

"No! You may not. It ain't none of your business." Ziggey responded sharply. Then, realizing that time was important and he couldn't go any further without this information, he backed off.

"It's personal, kid. I didn't mean to yell at you. We're workin' on a big European financing deal to make dozens of pictures. If word leaks out in this country, it could queer the whole deal. It ain't that I don't trust you, but you understand how these things work."

"Oh, sure. You can trust me. I won't even tell anyone that I did this for you." David said, relieved that he hadn't blown this opportunity.

"See ya a little after five then." Ziggey said standing and taking David's address that he had written on a napkin. "How long you think this will take?"

"I don't know. Depends how much is on the disc. If it's a double sided high density disc with one point forty four million mega bytes of..."

"OK, OK. See ya." Ziggey said already at the door.

It took less then ten minutes for David to print out the information on the disc. Ziggey removed each of the twenty pages as they came out, making sure that David did not catch a glimpse of what was printed. He immediately placed each page in a manila envelope without looking at it.

An offer of payment was declined by David as Ziggey took his leave and rushed back to his apartment.

What he saw astounded him. Each page was a dossier of one family. Included with information such as whether there were burglar alarms or watch dogs, Yoshi had listed the personal habits of the residents. If they had live-in servants, their days off, the kind of car the servants drove as well as the make and license numbers of the household cars.

What amazed Ziggey more than anything was that Yoshi had provided the combinations to many of the household safes and in some cases vaults where the stolen art and other treasures were hidden. This astonished him. Rich people must be really stupid, or Yoshi was even smarter than he thought.

The latter was true. Yoshi had simply applied his time honored tactic of giving a confidence and getting one or more in return. Yoshi brought these friends one by one to his South Hampton home, showed them a safe, gave them the combination and had them open it. He also had salted the safe with currency, giving the impression of millions of dollars in illegal cash.

They did the same in return, but as far as Yoshi knew and hoped, none of them had the foresight to change the combinations as he had done immediately after they left.

Yoshi had sold the idea of exchanging confidential information to his friends in the event of the death of one of them. Only they could trust each other with what they had illegally sequestered. They pledged that in the event of tragedy they would get to the booty before the IRS, their lawyers, or their accountants could, and hold it safe for the family.

So now Ziggey had more intelligence at his disposal then any outside burglar since Cary Grant in To Catch a Thief.

This was going to be easier than he thought. The only obstacle was gaining access to the homes.

34

As he read, he rated each house as to contents and accessibility. Some he dismissed. Others he starred. Yoshi had also indicated which homes where occupied as full-time residences, which were used weekends, and others that were vacant from October through May. The last you had to case carefully as sometimes one of the children showed up unexpectedly.

Ziggey was thrilled. Not going to be so hard. All he had to do was ingratiate himself under the guise of Executive Producer and the rest would be easy. He had seen the power of movie companies on location and the gullibility of civilians. Even rich civilians.

His only problem now, he thought, was making sure that Richard, Robert, and whomever else they brought on board were convincing movie-makers.

He still didn't have a script, but that didn't concern him. Robert had assured him that by tonight's meeting at Jimmy's he would present him with a first draft. And that, if he approved, he could have a shooting script within ten days.

Ziggey would approve. As long as it met two very important criteria. One it had to be shot on location in East Hampton, the target community. And two, it had to have enough material for the two weeks he planned to be there. As to the credibility of recognizable actors, Richard assured him that matters were well in hand. He already made some calls to agents advising them that he would soon be casting for a feature film using a variety of age ranges. And as soon as he got a final script he'd get back to them.

CHAPTER EIGHT

Seated at a back corner table in Jimmy's, Ziggey was euphoric.

"You just get some good news or something?" Robert asked.

"You betcha! I sure did." Ziggey replied, adding, "How's the script coming? I wanna get this thing on the road."

"Script is here as promised." Robert said handing Ziggey one hundred double spaced pages. "I think I outdid myself on this one. You sure are in a great mood. Want to share it with us?"

"Oh, yeah, sure." Again Ziggey fumbled for an appropriate answer without revealing his real reason.

"I just got some advance money from my backer, so you guys get some bread tonight. I told him you had the shorts and needed some dough to keep you going, and we needed to buy a few things."

This part was true. Ziggey had gotten ten thousand dollars from Mrs. Yoshi, but had told her nothing of his plan as agreed to with Mr. Yoshi. He asked and she simply had a messenger deliver the cash to his apartment in a super market bag filled with groceries. This, of course, had nothing to do with his state of mind. But it certainly helped both Richard and Robert as he handed each of them two thousand dollars.

"This should keep you guys going for a while. Told you we was gonna make some money. And this ain't nothin'.

Wait'll my buddy sells this thing. He's talkin' percentages and stuff like that."

Then Ziggey caught himself. He was over selling something that didn't need any more hype. Shut up schmuck, he said to himself. You're not running some street con here. This would be a good time to start acting like the movie executive you're supposed to be.

"Thanks." Robert said as he pocketed the money. "You'll notice I have, in addition to the script, something we call a treatment. It's only twelve pages long. It briefly tells the story. So if you and your partner like the idea, then I can polish the script."

"Why don't you just tell me about it? I'll read it later."

"Ok, sure." Robert would have preferred that Ziggey read it in private. That way if he or his backer didn't like it he wouldn't be embarrassed. Also, he hadn't told Richard anything about his idea thinking Richard might find the story line ludicrous. But what the hell, two grand for two weeks work wasn't bad, and there was more to come.

Trying not to look at Richard, he started. "Well, I got this idea a while ago. You may think it's totally nuts but I think it works, one hundred percent, commercially speaking that is."

Ziggey was getting fidgety. He didn't give a damn what the story was about, he would love anything, but he had to feign interest. He just wanted to get on with this. Time was becoming a problem. From the information he had, the best time for him to accomplish his ends was before Thanksgiving. Between Labor Day and Thanksgiving, East Hampton's rich were mostly absent, or only occasional visitors. Over the holiday season it got more crowded than would be convenient.

"I'm sure it works fine." Ziggey said. "Long as you got the one thing I asked for. Its gotta start in that rich town of East Hampton. Them foreigners still think America is paved with gold and that's what my friend wants 'em to see right up front."

"Oh, yeah. Absolutely. I did just that." Robert said with confidence. "You'll love it. I did exactly what you asked. The first two weeks of shooting take place on location right there. I don't know how familiar you are with East Hampton, but talk about your rich people..."

"Yeah, I know, I heard. Now let's hear what you got." Ziggey said getting impatient.

"Ok, here goes." Robert said, taking a deep breath. "Now this may be a little outrageous, but please hear me out and I think you'll like it.

A couple of months ago, I read this novel. Been Number One on the New York Times Best Seller list for over a year. Sold over four million copies in hard cover."

"Yeah. So?" Ziggey now annoyed, asked. "What's this got to do with your movie?"

"You're not proposing shooting 'The Bridges of Madison County,' are you?" Richard interrupted incredulously.

"No. Not exactly." Robert said with a wry smile.

"What the hell is the Bridges of whatever he said?" Ziggey asked getting more and more annoyed. He wasn't interested in a literary discussion, just some pieces of paper that would pass for a credible movie script.

Timidly, Robert continued. "Like I said, an enormous best seller that I found to be nothing more than melodramatic, totally unbelievable, romantic drivel. But what the hell do I know? Anyway, I got this idea to write a different ending. A "what if" this had happened, instead of what really did. I think it would be a great commercial success in this country as well."

"I can't wait to hear this." Richard said laughing.

"Cool it Richie! Let 'em talk." Ziggey said annoyed at Richard and relieved that Robert was finally getting to the story. "Sounds like you done good, Bobby. Let me hear it."

"OK. The book is about this middle-aged freelance photographer and this farmer's wife whom he meets while on an assignment in her rural midwest farm community. She's married with two teenage kids. Her husband and the kids are out of town for a week, as you might expect. There's insipid poetry, flowers, champagne, making it on the kitchen table and by bubbling brooks and crap like that.

"When he finishes his job he wants her to leave town with him, but she decides she has to remain loyal to hearth and home etc. etc. I've shortened it, but you get the idea."

"Yeah, I get it. But how do we get from this here farm to East Hampton? This I don't get." Ziggey said trying to remain composed.

"It's really quite simple, Ziggey. Let me continue. Suppose she did leave with him, they'd both find out fast that what was so ideal and exciting when it was an affair, wouldn't be so hot in the real world. I figured her husband probably commits suicide 'cause he can't stand the gossip and embarrassment in the small town. The son becomes a junkie. The daughter moves to LA and becomes a prostitute in Hollywood."

Ziggey interrupts. He isn't getting it.

"What the hell are you talking about? You nuts or something? All I wanted was some nice simple little movie about rich people in East Hampton. You got suicides, junkies, hookers. Shit! What's with you?"

"Let me finish. It all ties in beautifully." Robert said determined to go on and make his point.

"This I gotta hear." Richard said tears streaming down his cheeks, unable to control his laughter.

"The guy's next assignment is for a prestigious travel magazine. A pictorial of life on the Eastern end of Long Island. They want a contrast between the very rich and the

39

townspeople. How things have changed with the dwindling number of farms that had been sold to real estate developers who built multi-million dollar homes. So he decides he'll shoot in East Hampton, which has everything. So the movie starts with this couple very much in love in East Hampton."

"Now you're cookin'!" Ziggey yelled interrupting what had been for him an incomprehensible story line.

Robert pleased that his story was working, but put off by this interruption.

"I'm delighted you're pleased, Ziggey, but I would like to continue. It gets better and I think you'll particularly like the ending or rather choice of endings I've suggested."

"Yeah, sure Bobby. Go on. I didn't mean to interrupt or nothin' just I was so excited that you got exactly what I...I mean my backer wants. You done real good."

"OK, thanks. So as I was saying, they're in East Hampton where they're both exposed to a lifestyle they've never seen. They become the darlings of the rich. People take them into their homes, invite them stay with them. There's competition to see who has them as guests in their homes."

"That's great. Perfect, Bobby." Ziggey said holding his glass in a toast. "Just what the Doctor ordered. We get to see the insides of their houses, how they live and everything. I love it."

Richard didn't get it. He was confused by Ziggey's enthusiasm.

Ziggey had wondered how he was going to be able to get inside more then one home and this solved the problem.

Not that he gave a damn, but Ziggey, in the interests of his continued support, asked Richard how he liked the idea.

Richard, not one to look a gift horse in the mouth, particularly at this time, was temperate, but positive about the idea.

40

"Sounds good to me. I think it meets the criteria of your partner. Let me have a breakdown of the characters, Robert, and I'll start casting right away. Course we still have one major problem to solve."

This comment forced Ziggey and Robert to lower their glasses.

"What? What's the problem?" Ziggey asked.

"We need a director. I've been in a few films, but I'm not a film director and neither is Robert. You do a play and I'm your man. But if you were thinking that I was going to direct you're wrong. It's not my cup of tea."

Ziggey hadn't thought about it one way or the other. However, he was relieved. "Not to worry my friend. We'll get a director. Gotta be thousands of 'em running around the city looking for work. Now let's have a toast to this here movie we're gonna make."

"Excuse me gentlemen, I don't mean to interrupt but..."

The three of them looked over, surprised, at the young man who appeared from nowhere standing at their table.

Ziggey was not thrilled by this intrusion. "What'ya want kid? Can't you see we're busy? We're havin' a private meetin' here."

"Yes sir, I know that. But I couldn't help but overhear. I wasn't snooping or anything like that, but I'm sitting in this booth right next to you with my girlfriend, and well, she told me to mind my own business but..."

Ziggey interrupted. "You maybe should take her advice kid. It ain't polite to listen to other peoples conversation." Menacingly adding, "It could get a person in a lot of trouble."

"Yes, I know that. But I think I may be able to solve a problem you spoke of a few minutes ago?" The kid continued with determination.

41

Richard, ever the gentleman, and not feeling threatened that some confidence might have been betrayed, suggested the kid say his piece.

"What is it kid? What problem do you think you could solve for us?" Richard asked.

"I'm your director. That is if you'll give me a shot at it. I don't have a lot of experience or anything, but I know I could do a good job." He went on, gaining momentum as he spoke, seeing that he had, at the very least, gotten their attention. Breathlessly he continued.

"I just got my masters degree from the NYU film school. Did real well. Had a three-point-five average. Studied editing and writing, but most of my efforts went into learning how to be a director. I won Director of the Year award every year I was in undergraduate school. And my Masters thesis film is going to be submitted to the Cannes Film Festival. So, I don't know if you'd even consider someone like me but, maybe if you can't use me for this film I'd like to, at least, submit my resume to your Human Resources Department for something down the road. I'll do anything. I mean, even though my strength is in directing, I'd be willing to start as an assistant director. You wouldn't be sorry you hired me."

They just looked at each other. Richard and Robert admired his chutzpah, but one didn't hire a kid right out of college to direct a feature film no matter how small the budget.

Then Ziggey who had been listening intently, said to the shock of all, "Pull up a chair kid. Let me buy you a drink. You got a job! I like your moxie."

Robert shocked by Ziggey's naiveté said, "Ziggey I'm sure he's as bright and hard working as he says he is, but come on. We're talking feature film here, not some sixteen millimeter student film. I don't think it's a good idea."

"What're you talking about? I think we got us a budding star director here. You know, guys like us gotta give the next generation a shot."

Both Richard and Robert while remaining unconvinced of the wisdom of this decision, decided to keep quiet. It was Ziggey's money.

Neither knew why Ziggey did what he did.

"You just gotta remember one thing kid." Ziggey said putting his arm around the young man's shoulder. "I'm the boss. Whatever I say goes. I don't want no bullshit from you. You do whatever Robert or I tells you. You got that?"

The kid was practically in tears as he nodded affirmatively. "Could you excuse me a minute? I want to tell my girlfriend. Two months out of school and I'm directing a major motion picture. I can't believe it. Wait'll I tell Dave."

CHAPTER NINE

It was the second week in October now and Ziggey was getting antsy. A very productive week had passed since hiring "The Kid" Director in spite of Richard's continuing objections.

Robert felt it was not the most prudent choice, but had faith in the abilities of someone young and energetic. He also wasn't going to do anything to blow this golden opportunity for himself.

At the very least Patrick Stone, "The Kid" (no relation to Oliver Stone, a fellow NYU alum) was bright and had the technical knowledge. And they would still have ultimate control.

Robert had gotten to know and like Patrick over the last week while working together day and night on the shooting script and getting ready for production.

Patrick was twenty-three, had long reddish brown hair that he wore in a ponytail, five-ten, thin, horn-rimmed glasses and actually looked like a director. Who cared how young he was. He seemed to know his stuff, and Robert treated him with the same deference he would an older, more experienced director.

Richard would ultimately come around and Ziggey didn't really care. Not that Ziggey gave his decision a second thought.

Robert had explained that it was necessary to scout the locations that they were going to shoot. They would have to make arrangements with the city for police cooperation, get permission from homeowners, shopkeepers, and whomever else they might want to use.

He suggested, to Ziggey's horror, that if they didn't have one hundred percent cooperation in East Hampton it wouldn't be hard to find another community. Maybe in Connecticut?

"Make it work." Ziggey said as Robert and Patrick got into the stretch limo Ziggey had hired to take them to East Hampton at seven a.m. Monday morning. Ziggey knew full well that first impressions are everything. You are what you are perceived to be, and he wanted them to look and act successful. There was to be no doubt in anyone's mind that this was a viable company with plenty of money.

"Spread this around where ever you have to." He said handing Robert four banded stacks of one hundred dollar bills. "Make 'em love us. Want us. Can't wait for us to come. If you need more bread, let me know. This is where we gotta shoot." And as his final argument would tolerate no rebuttal. "It's where my backer wants us to shoot." No East Hampton, no movie. You got it?"

"I got it!" Robert said fingering the money, and rising to the hype. "They're gonna love us! I'll see to it. By the time you arrive I'll have them convinced it's the Second Coming. Now let me make sure I have everything."

Ziggey had given Robert a map of East Hampton with certain streets marked in red. He was to negotiate with every home owner on these streets for possible interior locations. Ziggey, of course, knew which ones he really wanted, but this would cover him and not make anyone suspicious.

When Robert questioned how he knew what streets he wanted, Ziggey answered with the standard, "That's what my backer said to do. He knows the neighborhoods and sez these is the most impressive."

So Robert, and the overjoyed Patrick were on their way to what they believed to be a burgeoning movie career. And in just the luxurious manner Patrick had always envisioned big shot movie people traveled.

45

Robert was going to make living arrangements for cast and crew. He would also introduce this young director as a genius. A wunderkid who had done amazing documentary work. Who the hell would know? As far as Robert could figure nobody ever saw a documentary.

Meanwhile back in the city, Richard was casting. He would love to have played the part of the forty-five year old male lead, but neither his physic nor his gray hair would allow him to play that young. So he followed orders. "Find actors that were immediately recognizable."

Richard opted for television actors. There were many who had short-lived but major roles on sitcoms and prime time dramas. When their shows were canceled some would stay in California for a while hoping for another role.

Those from New York returned in the hopes of Broadway, commercials, or a part on one of the five daytime soap operas produced in the city. Some wound up doing off off Broadway. But mostly they were out of work. It would take very little to get anyone of them to agree to any kind of movie deal.

Ziggey in the meantime was busy committing as much of the information from the disc to memory as he could. It was a lot to absorb and he didn't want to forget anything. The slightest detail overlooked could mean failure. Not to mention a long time in jail.

Included on the dossiers was a floor plan for each house or business. He had each of these letter-size dossiers reduced to type so small as not to be readable by the naked eye. Someone seeing this would simply perceive it as a series of black dashes.

He burned the original sheets and made sure that the disc was always on his person. When the job was over that too would be destroyed.

Ziggey did not need to wear glasses although he had quite a collection of non-prescription windowpane ones that served him from time to time to alter his look. Now he would need glasses. He had two pairs of bifocals made of high power magnifying glass. He liked these for two reasons: the first because of the obvious need to read the small print, the second was he thought they made him look more serious and prosperous.

The last thing Ziggey had to resolve, before leaving town, was his choice of fences. It wouldn't do to make phone calls through a switch board from a motel in East Hampton.

Ziggey's choice was Frankie, a guy, who had never served any time. He had a full-time job in a liquor store in the Village. He only fenced the occasional large item. He was smart enough to conceal this from everyone but his closest friends. Too many people he knew would make a score and buy a fancy car or fur coat for their wives or girlfriends and get caught. People will only believe you hit the lottery once.

"So, Frankie we got a deal?" Ziggey said shaking Frankie's hand early the next morning.

"Sounds good to me, but you gotta assure me the exact time of your arrival. I ain't hanging around no freakin' airport. I'm in and I'm out. I'll give you fifteen minutes, that's all. If you ain't there, I'm history." Frankie said with great conviction. Then laughing, continued. "I figured all this 'going straight' stuff I've been hearing about you was a crock. No way, I sez to myself, is ole Ziggey gonna tow the line. Had to be some scam with this movie crap. Wanna tell me about it?... Nah, never mind, better I shouldn't know. Not that you'd tell me anyway."

"You're right. Just know this. You ain't ever gonna see ole Ziggey after that night. I'm getting my "fuck you money" and I'm outta here." He stopped himself before he revealed anymore. "You'll be hearing from me with date, time and exact location. Don't confirm it. Just be there. You won't be disappointed. Believe me!"

CHAPTER TEN

Patrick had never been to East Hampton and was almost as excited about visiting there as he was about making his directorial debut.

"I've heard a lot about the Hampton's from some guys I knew at school." Patrick interrupted Robert who was going through pages of notes. "Is it as beautiful as they say?"

"Maybe better." Robert answered putting down his notes. "How come you were never there? Thought all you NYU film students were rich kids?"

Patrick laughed. "Not this one. I had to work my ass off to stay in school. Cost a fortune.

"Sometimes I held down three jobs at the same time. I delivered Pizzas for Jimmy, worked in a news store. Don't you recognize me? I waited on you several times. I knew who you were the minute I saw you in the restaurant."

"No, sorry. Didn't any of your rich friends ever invite you to the Hamptons?"

"Yeah, sure I was invited, but I could never go. Always had to work."

"What about your father? Couldn't he help? What's he do anyway?" Robert asked, fingering his notes, anxious to return to work, more to be polite then out of sincere interest.

"He's dead. Died my second year of undergraduate school. I was lucky to be able to stay in school. Got some student loans that I have to start paying off next year. I'm looking at five, six hundred a month in payments."

"Well then." Robert said opening his appointment book. "Let's you and I make sure the movie is a success. Here's a list of appointments I've made for the next two days. We're gonna work our asses off, but I have good feelings about this. I haven't exactly been raking in the big bucks myself the last few years so I want this to work as much as you."

Robert kept looking at his watch. He had arranged to host a noon luncheon for the members of the Chamber of Commerce, and didn't want to get off on the wrong foot by being late. This stretch of highway was notorious for long delays.

If all went well they would be checking into the Cozy Cabins Motel on the Montauk Highway just four miles from downtown East Hampton by ten a.m. They could freshen up and Robert would have time to brief Patrick further as to what behavior he expected from him.

The Cozy Cabins Motel is a group of single and double occupancy wood frame cabins set off the highway in a stand of beautiful old oak and beech trees. This would be an ideal setting, Robert thought, to keep cast and crew together in a rural setting outside of town. Not that East Hampton was known for its night life which, save for a few bars, was limited in the off-season.

Robert pointed out landmarks as they drove through the charming villages of Water Mill, Bridgehampton, and Wainscott.

"Did you ever live out here?" Patrick asked.

"No, but I'd like to. Just visited a lot," answered Robert.

"So you must know some people here. Should make things go easier?"

"I know a few. That's how I got this meeting scheduled on such short notice. That, and the fact that they love the idea of using their town as a backdrop for a movie. Especially the merchants. We're gonna spend a ton of money. They wouldn't see this kind of money till next summer, so cooperation shouldn't be a problem. But people can be funny. Some blue-haired old lady might not like the idea of movie company trucks blocking her driveway for fifteen minutes. We'll see. That's why I want to meet with the Chamber of Commerce first. Most of the members are also shopkeepers and have a lot of clout."

The greeting from the owner of Cozy Cabins was as hoped for. Having stayed there before, Robert knew the off-season rate for a single was forty dollars a night. Consistent with Ziggey's admonition that he wanted to "own the town" Robert offered to pay, in cash, the summer season rates which were double. He explained that they wanted to take over the whole compound and would want complete privacy. And that they were going to provide their own uniformed security. In addition, he would give them a cash security deposit. This unnerved the elderly owner who assumed the worst of movie people. The owner said that he wouldn't stand for drugs or drunken orgies. Although he seemed more than willing to take that risk, considering the cash offer.

Robert explained they weren't that kind of company. This was, by Hollywood standards, a film produced by conservative people. The security was going to be there as much to protect his property as that of the movie company's. To wall off trespassers and the curious, as well as thieves.

Patrick assumed that he and Robert would share a double cabin and was surprised when Robert assigned him his own. "You'll need your own space. Wouldn't look right if the director of a major motion picture had to share his room. Would it?"

"No. I guess not." Patrick said. "But I don't mind if you want to save some money. I've had roommates all my life."

"You're gonna have to work your ass off. You'll need the privacy. Listen, just 'cause this is a low budget film, doesn't mean we're not adequately funded. Ziggey assured me of that. So enjoy."

50

Robert wanted this luncheon in as public a place as possible, choosing a pub right in the center of town. There were three other restaurants in the area, but this one was virtually at the intersection of East Hampton's two main shopping streets. It ran perpendicular across the end of a charming cobble-stoned alley lined with shops. It was also next to the Chamber of Commerce building so they would be seen coming and going.

Robert had reserved the entire side room which was all glass and looked out over a parking lot. More exposure.

At eleven-thirty he had their driver pull the stretch limo in front instructing him to leave the car where it was. During the summer months, not much notice would be made of any luxury car, but now it would stand out. Something had to be going on. Of course after this luncheon -- and hopeful support -- word would spread like a California wildfire.

It couldn't have gone better. In addition to members of the Chamber of Commerce, Robert had invited the Police and Fire Chiefs, and the owner of the local newspaper, hoping to resolve any problems immediately.

Most members seemed almost euphoric, which surprised Robert. The scant resistance was quelled by those delighted with the prospects.

What Robert didn't know, and found out later from Patrick, was that just last week the town had its annual East Hampton Film Festival. The event had been entered into with much controversy, dividing many of the townspeople. Patrick had read about it in Variety and just assumed that Robert knew.

Those who were so receptive at the meeting delighted in "I told you so's" to the nay sayers, convinced as they were that the publicity from the festival had brought this movie company to town. Of course nothing could have been further from the truth, but he sure as hell wasn't going to let them know that. There would be people tripping over each other to help. To prove what incredible foresight they had.

Robert was giddy with what was happening as he returned to the motel. He finally was going to make it in the "biz". And even better than he could have imagined. Producer, writer and actor! He had already made it clear to Ziggey and then to Richard that he wanted a small part in the film. Not anything that would take him away from his other responsibilities too long.

Life was finally wonderful.

CHAPTER ELEVEN

As pre-production arrangements continued in East Hampton, Ziggey was enjoying similar success in the city.

Ziggey's luck continued beyond expectations. Maybe, he thought, that old fool in the park was right. God was with him on this one. It was about time.

Ziggey wasn't one of those New Yorkers afflicted with second-guessing good fortune. Ziggey went with the flow. If it went well it was meant to go well. The plan was obviously right. It was his time.

He had found just the man he was looking for without looking. A man with impeccable credentials. The Fence extraordinaire.

Frankie the fence had gotten a call from a friend informing him that a real hot shot was due in from Los Angeles this week. Apparently networking goes on in the fence business as well as in more legitimate enterprises.

Gary Gordon was a former movie actor turned criminal. He'd had a promising soap opera career going for him when his character was abruptly killed off the series.

This unexpected act, not only left him bitter, but also broke. Typical of so many rags-to-riches types, he had lived well beyond his income. Like a lot of actors he'd spent his gross income never worrying about things like taxes or what would happen if he lost his role. After a couple of successful years on a daytime soap most thought the gravy train would go on forever. They would save next year, now they had to live up to their self-perceived image.

Gary's story line had him in a coma in a hospital. He loved it. Bragged about how he got the same money and just had to lie there. No lines to memorize, no wardrobe, and no make up save for the bandages that covered all but his eyes.

While in this condition there was a major shift in management. A new Executive Producer with a big broom swept out the entire writing staff and brought in her own. This happened over a weekend so no one in the cast was aware of the change. Gary's writing Rabbi was gone and the new team didn't see his role generating rating points. He was just another six foot two, thirty-something, vapid blond hulk.

In his opening scene Monday, the CRT monitor above his hospital bed went from a pulsing beeping graph to a straight line hum. Gary heard this assuming that a code blue would be called and he would be saved by his doctor and lover. After thirty seconds, a long time in daytime TV, he got worried.

When neither the crash cart nor nurses showed up he panicked and raised his head yelling, "Hey what the hell is going on here?"

The director simply said from the control room over the public address system. "That's a wrap for you Mr. Gordon. Thank you."

Gary couldn't understand what happened even though he had heard of similar things happening to others. After a week of self-pity and indulgence he had his agent contact all the other soaps. But no one would touch him. He had been blackballed as being uncooperative. Seems the new Executive Producer was someone he had scorned several years ago. He not only had a brief affair with her but also her sixteen-year-old daughter. He was, as they say, dead meat.

Hollywood is a funny town where it is not uncommon for celebrities to pal around with people on the fringe of society. It's chic and sometimes dangerous, which appeals to those with a taste for the melodramatic. Usually not hard-core felons, but most knew where they could buy drugs, a weapon, or gamble illegally.

It was this crowd that Gary fell in with. Desperate for money to maintain his lifestyle, he succumbed to a little high class drug trafficking. His suppliers were not fools, they knew his condition, they had seen all this many times before. It wasn't hard to hire high class dealers.

When someone would ask what he was living on, he simply lied and said, "Are you kidding? Do you have any idea what kind of money I get from residuals? Why the European re-runs alone will keep me in gravy for years." This, of course, was not true. There were no local residuals as the daytime soaps don't re-run, and true there were foreign runs, but the pay only came to about twelve thousand a year. Hardly enough to sustain a Beverly Hills life. It was perfect cover for the uninformed.

From this, with the help of some new friends, he graduated into stealing. He didn't commit the actual thefts himself; he merely pointed out who had what and where it was that was worth stealing. He did verbally what Yoshi committed to the disc.

This was how he got in the business of Fencing. With his good looks, acting ability, and perceived wealth he was a natural to be used for transporting stolen property. It wasn't long before he was making regular runs to Europe, South America, and the Orient with stolen art, gems, and other items that couldn't be sold in America.

He was going to be in New York City just one night en route to Europe. Gary made it a practice never to spend one minute longer than absolutely necessary in any one place.

A meeting was arranged with Ziggey. They would meet outside the Sheridan Square subway station in the crowded center of Greenwich Village at eight o'clock that night. They would walk through some of the quieter side streets

55

where Ziggey hoped he would strike a deal with this highly recommended Fence.

"I'm gonna have a lot of stuff." He told Gary. "Real first class. We ain't talkin' ten caret gold chains here, we're talkin' a fortune in gold coins, stamp collections worth a fortune, gold bars, custom-made diamond jewelry, some uncut stones, and lots more. Lot of the stuff is illegal. I'm told by my connection that you're the guy to handle this."

Gary had heard this kind of line before and wasn't impressed, but he was interested. He always listened. The most unlikely source would occasionally come up with a big score.

Gary's interest was now peaked as he interrupted. "Let me make sure I understand, some of what you're going to steal hasn't been come by with bona fide bills of sale. Is that correct?"

"You got it. Perfect scam! Ain't none of them sons of bitches can blow the whistle. Not a word. They just gotta bite the bullet, keep their mouths shut and we're home free. That is, if you think you can handle it?"

Gary was delighted. It had become one of his specialties, but he didn't want to appear too elated. "Right up my alley." He said shaking Ziggey's hand. "Where and when? I'm going to be gone for a few days." He didn't say where never telling anybody his travel plans including, and especially, those he was fencing for. "How do I get in touch with you?"

"I ain't worked out the exact date yet." Ziggey said, "Won't know that for about ten days, then I'll get in touch with you."

"That's not how it works, my friend. I get in touch with you. You give me the exact time and spot the transfer takes place. I mean the exact time. I never wait. And we never talk again. I deal with someone only once. One deal per customer. That way there's no history of doing business. You got that?"

"Got it. Fine with me." Ziggey said. "You know how to find Frankie?"

"No, but my friend does. When you told Frankie you needed a specialist, someone with international experience, he got us together, didn't he? You let Frankie know when you're ready to hear from me and you will." Gary said, leaving Ziggey alone on the street as he disappeared back into the crowded streets.

CHAPTER TWELVE

Casting for the major roles had gone well for Richard. There was certainly no dearth of applicants. He had made arrangements with his acting school for the use of their theater for casting calls. Word had spread quickly and there were long lines every day.

Richard would not make final casting decisions without Patrick. Even though he still didn't have much faith in Patrick as a feature film director he knew that the appearance of the director making final casting decisions was important. Not that actors automatically respect a director. But this should work. They weren't hiring stars or for the most part even actors that still had agents.

Richard's opinion of Patrick was soon to change. Upon his return to the city from the meetings in East Hampton, Patrick was as fully prepared as any director Richard had ever worked with. His script was ready for shooting, marked in the practical and money-saving manner of shooting all the scenes that took place in one location at the same time even though out of story sequence. He had the air and manner of a seasoned professional.

Richard was not a man opposed to change, only slow to accept it. Patrick's actions plus a reassuring call from Robert praising the young mans professionalism and maturity was making a believer out of him. This might just work out after all, he thought.

Before Robert and Patrick left for East Hampton they had made all the arrangements in the city for equipment and truck rentals. Cameras, lens, lights, generators, raw stock (film), boom microphones, and tape recorders were all paid for and held for them.

Patrick was the proverbial kid in a candy store as he went through the rental company's stockroom picking out anything and everything he wanted. A far cry from his school days of having to get away with as little equipment as possible. As far as he could tell there were no budget constraints. Robert never said no to anything.

"Remember," he told Patrick, "After our two weeks shoot in East Hampton we will be coming back to the city to shoot here. So try and keep it as light as possible."

Two things surprised Patrick; one was that Robert paid in cash. He counted out thousands of dollars in hundred dollar bills to Patrick's awe.

The other was that Ziggey's apparent lack of interest in all that he and Richard and Robert were doing. Roles were being finalized and Ziggey didn't even want to look at the headshots of those they chose. Thousands of dollars were spent on rentals and he didn't want to see receipts. This was strange behavior for an Executive Producer he thought, but again dismissed it. He wasn't going to kill the Golden Goose. Nevertheless it troubled him. Nagged at his sub conscious.

It also struck Robert as odd, having had network experience where every dime had to be estimated, re-estimated, and accounted for almost on a daily basis. But he too wasn't going to let any suspicions fester into a confrontation that might cost him this unbelievable opportunity. So he decided to fully accept the terse explanation Ziggey had given him at the start. The same explanation he used for everything. "This is the way my backer wants it."

Ziggey had business cards made at a friend's small printing company. A service he'd used many times in the past, depending on who he wanted to be at the time. The address was fictitious and the phone number that of an answering service he hired for one month. If someone did call, the service would answer, "You've reached ABZ Productions. There is no one in the office at the present time. May I take a message?"

Ziggey knew that most people don't listen very well, a primary reason for his success as a con man. They hear what they want to hear, and in choosing ABZ, he knew most would think it was ABC they were hearing thereby giving him the credibility he wanted.

In addition, he had huge signs made to cover all the surfaces of the Ryder trucks where the Ryder logo appeared. "Another film by ABZ Productions"; "ABZ Production Company"; "ABZ Films".

There was a temporary sticking point with the equipment rental company who wanted their drivers used. But Ziggey got around that by having Robert introduce them to the drivers that Ziggey had hired showing them false Union IDs. That, and a huge cash security deposit won them over.

Ziggey didn't want a bunch of strangers hanging around with time on their hands. He wasn't concerned about the actors or the few production kids that Patrick hired. They were too full of themselves and would be too busy. But truck drivers had nothing to do but drive from spot to spot then sit all day and gossip.

He had plans for these trucks that would not be consistent with the logic of film production and would make the professional drivers suspicious.

His friends knew to do what they were told. No questions asked. Besides he had ulterior motives for hiring these men. Plans that went beyond driving. They were to serve as uniformed security guards and other duties that would be explained when the time came.

The only thing that troubled Ziggey through all these past weeks of preparation, was a twinge of guilt for involving his friends Richie and Bobby in both a lie and a crime.

It was a feeling exacerbated as the weeks went by due to the expectations these men had for this great opportunity. He had never seen Bobby so happy, so dedicated. And Richie, although the less demonstrative of the two was, clearly enjoying every moment of his new job.

He did not concern himself with the kid director. Ziggey stayed away from him as much as possible, not comfortable with his youthful exuberance which he mistook for arrogance.

However, he rationalized this two ways. One being that they were not actually going to do any of the stealing. They would only be innocent bystanders and therefore, he assumed, not culpable. The other was he planned to share some of his new wealth with them. He would make it up to them. Maybe not right away, but eventually. They would never have to worry again. In the end they would thank him, he convinced himself.

CHAPTER THIRTEEN

Richard, Robert, Patrick, cast, and crew arrived as planned on the Friday before the Sunday that Ziggey would show up in East Hampton.

Ziggey had emphasized, to the point of annoyance, how important it was that they not only be well received by the community, but embraced.

There was to be a huge party that Sunday night to kick off the big picture. It would start at five p.m. with cocktails and hor d'oeuvres and continue with a buffet as late into the night or early morning as people wanted to stay.

Everyone was invited. Not just the movers and shakers, but literally everyone within the town limits of East Hampton. A full page ad had been taken out in the East Hampton Star on the prior two Thursdays, its weekly publication day. Notices had been placed in all the local shops and the A & P.

They knew they could expect a huge turnout as the ad also stated in bold type that this was to be a casting party as well for the many extras they would need for the film.

"All types, All Sizes, All Ages Needed! From Infants to Senior Citizens! Meals and transportation provided. And!! Screen Credit For All Those Chosen."

It worked. There had been other movies shot in and around this location, but never an open casting call. Some locals had appeared as extras, but did not receive screen credit.

The idea was Robert's. He knew how people would react having worked briefly as an extra years ago before getting his first speaking role. There was virtually nothing some people wouldn't do to see themselves on film or TV.

As hoped for, hundreds of people showed up at the chic huge restaurant in its own building on a side street one block from the train station and walking distance to Main Street.

Normal capacity is on the order of one hundred fifty people. When it became impossible to fit one more person inside, Robert had the party moved outside to a courtyard and the parking lot. It was a madhouse spilling from the parking lot all the way across the street to the parking lot of a grocery store. Police had to be called for crowd control, which wasn't difficult as most of the small force was in attendance anyway.

Even though off-season, there was a growing population of year-round residents. It was now not uncommon to drive along country lanes and private roads near the ocean and discover lights on and cars in the driveways of every third or fourth mansion. Many had found, with the advent of fax machines, computers, and modems, that they could work here much of the time, only going to the city for an occasional meeting or business dinner.

So in addition to the townspeople; merchants, school teachers, hospital personnel, gardeners, and tradesmen, the party had attracted an upscale crowd as well.

This was perfect as the script called for shooting scenes in and around some of the estates. Getting permission to shoot on some of these properties should be easier now.

Robert and Richard mingled, doing their public relations best hyping not only the movie, but the arrival of the Executive Producer. The eccentric, "diamond in the rough," brains behind this production company.

Patrick ingratiated himself with everyone. Mothers were calling daughters not in attendance to hurry over.

Everyone, it seemed, had someone he should meet either for romance, a part in the movie, or both.

The principal actors were reveling in the attention they had missed so much over the past years.

For them, as for Robert and Richard, this was their return to show business. Albeit not a Stephen Spielberg production, but nonetheless a bona fide feature film. A film with great artistic potential. One they were given to understand should gain great critical acclaim if not great box office. So they all believed.

Patrick had hired friends of his from film school as crew. None was over twenty-five years old.

All told, the crew numbered only fifteen people not counting Robert, Richard, and the driver/security people they were told Ziggey was bringing with him. A typical feature film or one-hour television drama would have a crew of forty to fifty people.

The enthusiasm of the cast and young crew at this party was infectious. The civilian community was getting as psyched as the players.

At exactly six p.m. Ziggey's white stretch limo pulled up in front of the restaurant followed by a caravan of trucks and cars all festooned with ABZ Production logos. There were two twenty-foot trucks carrying cameras, lens cases, tripods, lights, cables, generators and all the other heavy equipment. Also four nine-passenger vans that would be used to move cast and crew from location to location, and two four door sedans.

Robert had called Ziggey during the day informing him of the location of Cozy Cabins, assuming that the equipment and drivers would go directly there. He had made provisions with the owner for parking behind the cabins so as to eliminate, as he said, a circus atmosphere attracting every passerby. Even though it would only be a matter of minutes before every one in town knew where they were staying, it would be better not to create a fairground atmosphere.

So, no one was more surprised then Robert when this block-long caravan pulled in front of the restaurant.

Ziggey, of course, wanted to be seen. He wanted all the trucks to be seen. This was proof of the credibility of ABZ Productions and himself. The circus had come to town.

"Ziggey! Great to see you, but how come you didn't park all this stuff at the cabins? You had to pass right by them on the way here," Robert asked curiously as Ziggey climbed slowly out of his pretentious vehicle. "You did see them didn't you?"

"No." He lied. Ziggey knew every street, every alley way, and every private road in town unless something had changed since Yoshi had furnished him with the information. "Guess we musta missed it." he said brushing Robert aside surveying the crowd. "Man, this is some shindig. You done good, Bobby, real good!"

Ziggey had assumed, if not the language, at least the proper show business attire. Levi's, black turtle neck, worn under a black sport jacket, and black cowboy boots. He had watched enough television talk and interview shows, and read enough People Magazines to know how these clowns dressed. It was only a shock to Richard and Robert who had assumed no such affectations and had never seen their friend in anything but the most nondescript clothing.

But that was only half the story. Ziggey was also wearing a black baseball cap with large white ABZ letters embroidered in front. In smaller type, below the logo, Executive Producer was spelled out in red type.

Patrick had seen this convoy arrive and was fighting his way through the crowd with both of the movie's stars in tow. Before he got to the car he yelled out, "Mr. Zignorelli, Mr. Zignorelli," This made lots of heads turn. The much ballyhooed Producer was finally here and everyone wanted to meet him.

"Mr. Zignorelli, I want you to meet our two stars. This is Michael O'Neil who will be playing Robert Kincaid, and this is Heather Jones the woman he falls in love with. Michael meet Mr. Zignorelli."

Ziggey was still surveying the crowd, nonplused by this unnecessary introduction. "Nice to meet ya," he said without making eye contact.

"Heather this is our boss, Mr. Zignorelli. Mr. Zignorelli... Mr. Zignorelli say hello to Heather."

Annoyed at being tugged at the elbow by the overly enthusiastic Patrick, Ziggey decided to get it over with, made eye contact, and was very impressed with what he saw.

"It's my pleasure to meet you Miss...I'm sorry, I didn't catch the name."

"It's Heather, Heather Jones and the pleasure is all mine, Mr. Zignorelli."

"Ziggey. Call me Ziggey, that's what all my friends call me," he said while doffing his baseball hat and bowing.

Robert looked at Ziggey, then at Patrick, then back to Ziggey with shock. Ziggey's head was completely bald. What now, he thought as he escorted Ziggey through the crowd.

CHAPTER FOURTEEN

Ziggey didn't receive the same adulation as the actors, however, he got exactly what he hoped for. He was being pandered to by the rich of this community. Or at least many of the wives of the rich.

After being introduced to several people that Robert thought he should meet, and exchanging brief pleasantries, Ziggey dismissed Robert and positioned himself in the middle of a curved banquet in front of the fireplace in the center of the restaurant. He wanted to work this group alone.

Ziggey understood demographics and this was where his target group was congregated.

On the banquet and at surrounding tables were older, sedate, more substantial-looking folks.

"Everybody's havin' a good time I trust?" Ziggey asked no one in particular.

"Yes. Yes we are. Thank you. Are you one of the stars of the picture?" a woman asked.

Laughing modestly, Ziggey replied, "Oh no madam. I'm afraid I'm not that talented. I'm just the Executive Producer. It's my company that is doing this and I trust many more productions in this part of the country. I hope you can bare with us through this confusion? I hope this won't be too disruptive of your lifestyles."

"Don't be silly Mr....I didn't get your name sir."

"Ziggey, please just Ziggey. That's what my friends call me." he said, taking the woman's hand and kissing it.

On hearing that he wasn't an actor several members of the surrounding group moved in closer. These were people more interested in the money side of show business. Not star struck. At least not for the former daytime soap actors present. If Julia Roberts showed up it would be different.

Others were clearly impressed by being in the presence of a movie mogul.

"Where will you be staying?" asked another woman.

"I believe my staff has arranged to accommodate me at a place called the Cozy Cabins?" answered Ziggey. "I'm told it's quite charming."

"Not really, unless you like roughing it," Someone in the crowd said sarcastically.

"A man like you certainly shouldn't be staying there." said another.

And another, "It may be all right for your staff, but I'm sure you're used to living on a much grander scale."

"I have a great idea!" Mrs. Overdressed, Over Made-Up, chimed in.

"What's that?" Ziggey asked knowing exactly what she was going to offer.

"You can stay with me. I mean," she paused, a little embarrassed at her own enthusiasm in front of her friends. "I mean you can stay at my house. We have a perfectly lovely and spacious guest house right by the pool. Not that you'll be using the pool this time of year, but I think it would suit you perfectly and I would be honored to have you."

"That's very nice of you, but I don't want to impose." Ziggey humbly responded.

"You would be more than welcome at my estate," Another woman chimed in. "And you certainly wouldn't be an imposition. My husband is in Europe on business, and if I must say so, I can offer you the privacy I know people of your position seek."

"I don't know what to say. You're all so gracious, I'm almost embarrassed." Ziggey said while thinking, this is easier than I thought. Ain't been here one hour and they're eating out of my hand. Rich schmucks. The bidding wars for my attention have begun.

But Ziggey demurred. For now anyway. Now he wanted names and addresses. Tomorrow he would accept an invitation. The one that would best serve his interests.

CHAPTER FIFTEEN

Shooting started as planned Monday morning. Patrick and Robert set out with the crew to film a dawn scene over a large old farm that was the temporary home of migrating Canadian Geese. The characters of the freelance photographer and his new girlfriend were taking still photographs of this landscape while they, in turn, were being filmed.

Robert had not only convinced Richard and Patrick that his dark version of "what if" the book had continued would entice readers who wondered what would have happened if this couple had run off, but that the critics would love it.

The script called for the characters to spend two weeks in the Hamptons' on their first assignment, thereby satisfying Ziggey's requirement.

As this film version continued, life was better than anticipated for the still married Mrs. Johnson.

She quickly took to the offers of luxury accommodations and use of fancy cars. However, what she didn't realize, was that her rugged, photographer/lover hated all these trappings. He had lived a Spartan life by choice. By the end of the two weeks the fairly tale sex had stopped, and there was tension between them that she didn't understand. When confronted, his stoic silence was more than she could bear. Fights started, but nothing was resolved. She felt used. She was. His freedom was gone. He felt trapped. He was.

By the time the script called for them to leave the Hamptons' they were barely speaking. The script then called for them to meet with a magazine publisher in New York City regarding a new assignment. The drive to the city in his old battered pick-up truck was a far cry from the Mercedes and Bentleys that Mrs. Johnson had gotten used to and now craved.

They stayed one night in a squalid midtown hotel, a far cry from her well kept farm house. He got drunk that night and hit her in response to her complaining. She left before he awoke.

Not aware that her husband was dead, her son a junkie, her daughter gone, and the farm taken over by the county for taxes, she got on a bus and headed for what had been home. She would beg forgiveness. Do whatever was necessary to resume her mundane, but safe life.

Arriving home and learning the fate of her family, learning that her daughter had moved to Los Angeles, she was faced with the decision of whether she should look for her.

This is where Robert had left the story, the ending still not decided. Should she find her daughter, and live happily ever after in sunny Southern California?

Or should she wander in pursuit of an elusive past becoming old and dying before her time as a homeless street person?

No matter which choice he made, no one would leave the theater humming the tunes of this film.

Robert had obviously gotten bitter over the last ten years and saw this as his opportunity to prove that the grass wasn't always greener.

Richard thought the movie more dour than necessary, but kept his mouth shut. He opted for the ending with some hope, but he had a job. Also, he knew how fickle movie audiences and the pseudo intellectual movie critics were.

Both he and Robert knew that if the holier than thou New York and L. A. Times liked it, all the movie going sheep that hang on every review would see it. They'll probably sanction it as "a dark trip into the world of realty. A must see for everyone over the age of ten. Learn what life is really about." They both thought this was just the sort of movie the Times critics might love.

If there wasn't hunger and starvation in the world to write about, the New York Times would invent it.

Patrick, on the other hand, was ecstatic. Real life. Real drama he thought. His first job, directing a reality-based film. Of course this wasn't reality-based at all. But don't tell him that.

Ziggey didn't give a hoot. Never read the final script nor any of the drafts that Robert dutifully presented to him. Something that was becoming more and more apparent to Robert. He didn't get it. The Executive Producer should be more involved. Just what the hell was Ziggey doing anyway? What was he so busy with, if not the film?

Robert pondered this more frequently now. It was nagging at him more than he liked to admit. But like Richard, he had a job. And, like Richard, every week they received their salaries in cash. The best thing that had happened to him in years.

Ziggey, suddenly with access to all that money? Ziggey in the movie business? It didn't wash, in spite of the story Ziggey had told. Ziggey had been, after all, a professional criminal. Something one couldn't dismiss with ease.

So they went about the business of movie-making. The townspeople couldn't have been more cooperative. Actually, Robert thought, they were making bloody fools of themselves. These, so called, sophisticated rich people were slobbering all over everybody in the movie company to curry favor. It was laughable. And exactly what Ziggey hoped for.

CHAPTER SIXTEEN

After much cajoling and after weighing competitive offers, Ziggey let himself be talked into moving out of Cozy Cabins and into the home he had already selected. The house he chose, of course, was on Yoshi's list and, of course, the target house. The one with the great stolen art. Not to mention other highly coveted items.

Again, things were going so well that Ziggey was convinced that his time had come. Nothing could go wrong. He had never entered into a scam so thoroughly prepared nor with so much intelligence at his disposal.

If he ever had to resort to crime again, which he doubted, this was the path he would take.

The house was one of several on a private road with no exit, in an area called Georgica Pond. Some of these huge homes backed onto the ocean and others, the pond. All had private security alarm systems. There were no street lights, and if not for house lighting you would not be aware that anyone lived in this area.

It was perfect. This was Ziggey's headquarters. His benefactor's husband was in Europe, as she had said, the children were away at college, and save for the German Shepherd and one maid, they were alone.

Ziggey's suite was the third floor of this Spanish style twenty-room house. He had a bedroom, living room, and bath. Not bad, he thought. He could get used to this. Maybe he would after all.

From here, during the day, Ziggey could see two other target homes, both on this private road. Three others were on Lily Pond Lane, the road you took to get to the private road.

There were three others on roads that were perpendicular to Lily Pond Lane, one on a corner of Georgica Road, and two on Quail Lane next door to each other.

The house on Georgica Road was owned by a multi-millionaire publisher who led a predictable life. He was a bachelor that only came out weekends arriving between six thirty and seven Friday evenings, returning to his New York City town house on the four o'clock train Sunday afternoon.

Sometimes friends of his would use the house during the week, but rarely this time of year. A maid showed up once a week and stayed for only a few hours during the day. Her presence there was obvious by the parked pink motor scooter.

The house was modest by this neighborhood's standards, only six bedrooms and five baths in the main house situated on a modest one acre plot. In addition to the main house, set in the back of the property was a pool house consisting of one large room and bath.

This house was ideal, not for the treasures it would yield, but for three other reasons. One was location. It is approximately halfway between the other eight homes. Two, was that all but the peak of the roof was hidden from view by tall hedges and trees. And the third was that this schmuck had no security. Access to the main house was simply gained through an unlocked cellar door. And the pool house had no locks at all.

This house was to be the central receiving point for stolen goods.

The two houses on Quail Lane were next to each other. One owned by a movie star who was rarely there except for a few weeks in the summer, the other by the widow of a famous artist. She traveled a lot. This house and the one next door were protected, so they believed, by a private security company.

The house he was in and the ones on Lily Pond Lane would present more of a problem as they were occupied year round.

His first night in residence Ziggey's hostess threw a party. Since there was little social activity this time of year all those invited showed up.

This was to be a more intimate get together than the "Laundry Restaurant" party. Invited were the stars of the movie, along with Richard, Robert and Patrick, and thirty or so of her friends including neighbors on the private road. The only townspeople there were those working the party; caterers, bartenders, and servants.

The script called for a portrayal of how things had changed over the last twenty years from a largely farming and fishing community to an escape for the rich and pretentious. How former potato farms had been sold to developers who built million dollar tract homes. How the fishing industry was all but dead. And how many of the old timers resented these ostentatious, often rude, interlopers.

This story line played right into Ziggey's hands and was the only part of the script that he had paid any attention to.

The party gave Ziggey the opportunity to achieve another of his goals. Taking each of the target home owners aside, one at a time he thanked them for allowing the use of their homes for the movie.

"You don't know how much this means, not only to me personally, but to the success of my film." He told each one as they strolled by the pool. "I never had such cooperation before. It makes me feel humble that you'd accept us with such open arms. It's, I don't know how to say it... it's just so damn nice of you." He almost choked on his set speech.

"We're more than happy to help," "Consider our home your home." was the consensus's response.

However, the true point of these private talks was when Ziggey slipped in; "Listen, I don't want you to say anything to anybody else, I'm sure I can trust you." He said putting his arm around the shoulder of whomever he was addressing. "What I'm going to ask should not alarm you. Not to worry." Which of course put everyone on guard and made them worry. Continuing with, "I know my people. All of them seem trustworthy. But you never know. Sometimes the guy you least expect turns on you. Gets greedy. See something he just can't resist. You see what I'm sayin'?"

They nodded with trepidation not having any idea where he was going with this, but nervously hanging onto every word of this big shot producer waiting for the other shoe to drop.

"What I'm gettin' at, and believe me it hurts me to have to even suggest this, is that I believe it's in your best interests if while we're working in or around your magnificent estate, that you put all your valuables in a safe place in your house. Like, in a safe or something like that. Not that I'm the slightest bit concerned, but it would kill me if after we left you found something broken or missing. Not that I wouldn't make good on it, but I know for a fact that some things you just can't replace with money. I got a lot of stuff like that in my homes and it just scares the hell out of me every time I leave on business that it might get stolen or something. So like I always say, a pound of prevention could save you a ton grief."

Most had planned to or already done exactly as Ziggey had advised and thanked him for his concern. All were relieved and appreciative. These rich people and their new friend were bonding.

Ziggey, of course, just wanted everything organized. He wasn't going to have time to root around these huge homes looking for the booty on his list.

"Anyway," Ziggey concluded, "I didn't mean to make you worry. As you've already seen, I have my own private security force." He had two uniformed men stationed at the entrance to the house for effect. "These are guys I've known for years and trust them with my life. Been with me on every picture. They'll be stationed in front and back of your property whenever there is a crew working at your place. So again, not to worry."

These uniformed security people were his handpicked truck drivers now serving double duty. Nobody paid any attention to truck drivers, or security people, and wouldn't be able to pick one out of a line up if their life depended on it.

After his last tête-à-tête, Ziggey stayed by the pool for a moment, enjoying the calm while congratulating himself on how well things were going. How planning paid off. How stupid and gullible, even the most sophisticated people were when it came to being in the presence of show business people.

As he started back to the house he heard a noise from the guest cottage by the pool. At first he dismissed it assuming it was tree branches rustling against the roof. But then he heard a voice emanating from the cottage. He had to investigate.

What if, he worried, someone was living there that he didn't know about. Someone Yoshi's dossier hadn't covered.

As he stealthily made his way to a side window, he thought he heard a familiar man's voice. Then he heard what was unmistakably a woman's giggle. Then almost too loud he exclaimed, "Oh shit!" As he recognized the voice and knew exactly what was going on. His view through the sheer curtained window confirmed his suspicion.

Robert was making it with some young chick on the floor in front of the fireplace.

Damn! Got to put an end to this. Stupid horny son of a bitch could fuck up everything. Last thing I need is to have him getting involved with some broad. It wouldn't be so bad if she was one of the actress from the movie. That he could live with. But she wasn't. She had to be one of rich locals or she wouldn't have been at this party, he thought while trying to figure out a way to kill this romance.

He had to know where his movie people were at all times. If these people started socializing, visiting homes, shacking up, he wouldn't have the freedom that was all important to his plan. After all the careful analysis, the one thing that could screw everything up was to find someone in a house that should be vacant.

He left undiscovered, resolved to nip this thing in the bud. He would post a memo, he was dictating to himself as he walked, on every Cozy Cabin door in the morning.

"Company Policy. There will be no socializing with the people of the town unless I give permission."

He would take Robert aside first thing in the morning, find how who this chick was, where she lived, and order him to stop. He would explain to him that he was welcome to return, do what ever he wanted after the movie was finished, but he didn't want, wouldn't stand for such diversions. Should work? He thought. If not there was always money.

CHAPTER SEVENTEEN

The first week of shooting went well. The history of the Osprey nesting habits had been chronicled, the demise of the fishing industry, the real estate developers taking over most of the farm land all had been etched on film. And, as far as Ziggey knew, neither actors nor crew were dating locals.

He made his point emphatically the first thing the morning following the party. Robert, Richard and Patrick were told in no uncertain terms that this was one thing he would not tolerate from them or the staff.

"Aren't you over reacting a bit?" asked Robert "We're not a bunch of kids you know. We've been busting our butts. What's wrong with a little relaxation on our own time?"

Ziggey was surprised by the vehemence of Robert's reaction. "Me, over reacting? What the hell you got going with that broad anyway? Can't you keep it in your pants for a lousy coupla of weeks? Jeeze! How long you been seein' this chick anyway?"

"I met her the first day I got here, and she isn't just some broad. It's turned into kind of a thing." Robert answered a little defensively, surprised by Ziggey's anger.

"Well, do all of us a favor and cool it for another week. I don't give a shit what you do after the movies over, come back here and fuck your brains out. Marry her, have kids, and live happily ever after, but not now."

"I still don't get it Ziggey." Robert asked tentatively. "I've never seen you so adamant. But if that's what you want, I'll cool it, though it won't be easy."

"Fine, thank you." Ziggey said softening his demeanor. "I know you guys is adult and all that, it's just this thing is so important to me. To all of us. And I know myself from personal experience how a broad can screw things up. Now let's get back to work. I'll see you guys tonight. Got stuff I gotta do."

Why? kept nagging at Robert's brain all day. He still isn't taking an active part in the production, has no interest in seeing the rough-cut film of the previous day, and now this. Something's not Kosher here.

More troubling though was the fact that lust had turned more quickly than he could have imagined into the early stages of love. This was not a series of one-nighters strung together that would last only the duration of his stay in town.

Ziggey would shit, he thought, if he knew just how far this romance had progressed. Robert had been a dinner guest at Tiffany Cohen's parents house on three occasions. He had met her father a few days before the father had moved back to their Fifth Avenue condo and his law practice.

Tiffany and her mother, as they had done every year since she finished graduate school, would stay in this peaceful tourist-free community through the Thanksgiving holiday. Daddy would join them and then they would close the house till April of the following year. Robert was expected to join the family feast at Thanksgiving.

Robert was also invited to have lunch at "The City Club," with the prosperous Harold Cohen, Esq. a Senior Partner in the prestigious Wall Street law firm that bore his name, when he returned to the city. Seems Mr. Cohen not only liked him, but was prepared to offer legal and financial council. Along with litigation, and corporate law this firm had a small, selective entertainment department. They represented several substantial celebrities for endorsements, license agreements, and general legal work.

Robert didn't feel it necessary, at this time, to explain that financial advice was the last thing he needed. But who knew? To quote the song, "This could be the start of something big." Probably not with Ziggey, the voice in his ear kept reiterating, but this credit could help launch his dormant career.

With all the exteriors finished the first week, they were now scheduled to start shooting the interiors of homes and local businesses to portray how this community of such diverse people lived and worked.

At six a.m. Monday morning, assembled on the corner of Main Street and Newtown Lane were fifty extras huddled against buildings and in doorways to stave off the first portent of winter. The wind and freezing drizzle were awful, but they were all there. People had cups of coffee and tea in their hands provided by craft services, not to drink, but to keep their hands warm. Nobody was dressed for this weather as the scene was written to take place in the summer. Wardrobe called for Polo shirts, shorts, T shirts and the like. If it wasn't so ludicrous it would have been funny. Nobody hired for this menial job demurred, everybody froze, no one complained. They were in show business. They were going to be in the movies. It was worth risking pneumonia even if they weren't getting paid.

Robert had seen this behavior before in Hollywood. They're nuts. Extras will do anything, absolutely anything to be seen on the screen. But those he witnessed in Hollywood were paid professionals hired for some shows he'd worked on. These people weren't getting anything more than coffee, donuts and they think, screen credit. Go figure.

The days shooting was to go on in spite of the weather. Extra lighting had been employed to make it a bright summer day.

While munching on cold burgers from a local pub, Robert and Patrick were shocked to see Ziggey walking towards them on Main Street.

"Wonder what the hell he's doing here?" Robert said to Patrick.

"Don't know. Maybe he's got some scene changes." Patrick naively responded.

"Scene changes? You nuts? How could he change something he never read to begin with? Something's fishy here." Robert said, annoyed at this pending interruption.

"What do you mean something fishy?" Patrick asked worried.

"Don't worry about it. Hey, Ziggey, good to see you. What's up? Nothing wrong, I trust."

Robert had tread very carefully with Ziggey since his edict of No Dating. Not because he stopped seeing Tiffany, because he hadn't, but to get back in Ziggey's good graces and stay there, at least until this project was over.

"Everything's fine. Just thought it was about time I stopped by to see how you guys were doing. Feel a little guilty that I haven't taken a more active part, but I'm sure you understand, the life of an Executive Producer is one where you gotta wear a lotta hats. So, how's it goin'? Everything OK? You need any bread or anything?"

"No, thanks Ziggey everything is fine. Actually we're a little ahead of schedule which should make your backer happy." Patrick jumped in.

Distracted by something he was trying to focus on across the street, Ziggey didn't respond. Then he turned realizing it was Patrick who had spoken. "Yeah, kid everyone'll be happy." Ziggey's attention was again focused across the street. "Who's that guy over there?"

"Which one?" Robert asked.

"The one in front of the book store. The tall blond guy. Who is he?" Ziggey persisted.

"Oh, him." Robert answered. "Just an actor we picked up for a song. Small part. Used to be a big soap star. I don't even know his name. The guy made a ton of money then screwed up somehow. Now he's just happy to be working. Shitty business. He's playing the role of the bookstore manager." Robert continued as he fumbled with some papers. "You know him? Here wait a minute, I got his name on the call sheet."

Ziggey held his breath, afraid of the name he was now sure he would hear.

"Here, here it is." Robert said pointing to the name on the call sheet. "Gary Gordon."

"I don't fuckin' believe it." Ziggey said louder than he intended. Then to himself, "He can't be that fuckin' dumb. Nobodies that fuckin' stupid. Not even an actor."

"What don't you believe?" Robert asked concerned over the shocked look on Ziggey's face. "You know this guy?"

"Oh, no. I don't know him. I just said I can't believe how dumb some guys are. Hangin' on like that. No fuckin' self-respect. But I suppose if you have any you ain't gonna be an actor to begin with."

"Wait a minute, Ziggey, you forget that I'm an actor, Richard's an actor and so are some of your best friends at Jimmy's."

Ziggey was not paying any attention to Robert, concerned now with what appeared to be a serious problem. Ziggey's mind was racing. He'd have to get this schmuck alone. Find out his game. Just what the hell was he doin' here? Then the first of several conclusions occurred to him. Blackmail! Had to be. This greedy son of a bitch was gonna queer the whole deal if he didn't get a bigger cut.

Well, we'll see about that. His thoughts continued. I've been around the block a few times. No Hollywood type is gonna screw me outta what's rightfully mine.

"I gotta go. See you later." Ziggey said hurrying back to where he parked his borrowed Mercedes.

"Moody guy, isn't he?" Patrick said. "Guess there's a lot more pressure in being an executive producer than I realized?"

"Yeah, I guess so." Robert answered, the cerebral nagging getting worse.

CHAPTER EIGHTEEN

"What the fuck are you doin' here? I couldn't believe my eyes. You wanna blow everything?" Ziggey asked in a furious whisper while pinning Gary against the wall of his Cozy Cabin room at three in the morning. "You outta your fuckin' mind? Or what?"

Ziggey was stronger than his physique suggested and Gary was worried.

"Calm down. Will ya? For Christ's sakes. Let go of me. You crazy or something? What am I doing here? I'm an actor. I'm in the damn movie. What the fuck are you doing here?" Then, looking down at Ziggey's bald pate, he couldn't help but laugh.

"What's with the bald head?"

"None of your fucking business," he answered releasing his grip as he realized that Gary had no idea that this was his movie.

"I'm the God damn Executive Producer of the God damn movie. It's my fuckin' movie you're in."

"You gotta be puttin' me on. I don't believe it." Gary said.

"Believe it! Mr. Actor."

"How the hell was I to know? You never told me anything about any movie."

"It never occurred to me to tell you nothin'. Why should it?" Ziggey said.

"You're right." Gary said. "What happened was; my old agent called. He heard about this flick and thought it might be a shot for me to start over again."

"What the hell do you need to act for? It don't make no sense."

"For credibility and mobility. People still think I'm living off all the money I made in TV, but that was a long time ago. I heard rumors. Some folks were getting suspicious about how come I still live so well. Where's the money coming from? Some know that residuals don't last forever. So, I figured this would be a good shot. Maybe get my name in the papers again. Maybe get more small parts, different locations around the world. I have international contacts as you know. I figured this film would logically have me on the East Coast ready for our deal."

"OK, OK. I get it. And don't really give a shit. Just stay away from me. When are you finished here?"

"Tomorrow."

"Good, then get the hell out of town. Friday is D day. Leave a phone number and address with Richard, the casting guy. Tell him you want to work for him again or something like that. You'll hear from me." Then Ziggey left by the same window he had entered. His confidence and recent belief in God were waning. He didn't like this one bit.

He got into his car, letting it roll down the slight incline of the parking area before starting the engine at the edge of the highway. Sleep was the farthest thing from his mind as he headed for town. Thinking it was too bad he wasn't in the city instead of this hick town. There he could go to any number of bars that would let him in even though they were closed to the public. Besides he had another problem, he couldn't go back to his estate without disturbing the damn watchdog. So he decided to drive around till dawn, check on his targets, and find a diner someplace and drink coffee. There were still working fishermen in Montauk down the highway that would be up having breakfast.

Cruising by each of his target homes and concentrating on his plan, for the moment, erased this nights unfortunate discovery. He was pleased that all was in place. In front of or nearby each house was an ABZ vehicle. Some vans, or panel trucks, others four door sedans.

This was part of his plan. He had ordered rentals of more vehicles than they needed. The reason being he wanted his company's trucks and cars to be as common and as accepted as a gardener's pick-up truck. He reasoned, correctly so, that after a few days, no one, not even the cops, would pay the slightest attention to seeing an ABZ logo any time, any place, any hour of the day. This was another thing that struck Robert as curious.

When a couple of people did ask, they were told that they were there to prepare for the next shoot, or some such. It didn't matter, these were movie folks and anything they said was believed.

So far so good. Maybe he shouldn't worry about Gary, after all, he was a professional. One of the top men in his field. It wasn't in his interest to jeopardize the hugely profitable outcome. So for now Ziggey put this slight curve in the road out of mind.

Continuing on his way east to Montauk on route 27, Main Street in East Hampton, he was feeling relieved. While he was waiting for a traffic light in town to turn green, he caught a reflection on a plate glass window in a wide shopping alley to his right that ended with a pub across the back. Something about this image bothered him. It looked like people. Were these some of his people leaving this saloon at this hour? He really didn't give a damn if it was cast members, but were they possibly his security people, neè: truck drivers. Were they plastered and talking too much? Not that they knew of his plans, but a revelation of their backgrounds would quickly arouse interest in this small town. He was sweating with the paranoia of a criminal. A feeling he remembered all too well from the past.

Calm down, he told himself while wiping his brow. Who cares, I'm outta here in four days. However, the car turned to the right as if on its own and stopped in a parking lot that had a view only of the back of the pub.

"Shit this ain't no good." Gotta drive by the front again. As he edged the car out of the lot as quietly as he could, he caught sight of someone squeezing between a parked car and dumpster behind the pub.

"What the fuck?" He said out loud. "What the hell is that little son of a bitch doing here?" He re-parked the car and ducked below the steering wheel so as not to be discovered.

The figure was backing away with something on his shoulder. As it passed under a street light it was clear that it was Patrick holding a video camera.

Ziggey watched unseen as Patrick walked towards Main Street. He decided to follow at a distance. Patrick crossed Main Street and headed down Newtown Lane. It wasn't hard to follow him as no one else was on the street. The only problem was his being seen, but Ziggey was good at this sort of thing.

As Ziggey crossed Main Street, he was startled by voices he heard behind him. They were coming from the shadows in the pub's alley. What the hell was going on? Who were these guys and why was Patrick video taping them?

Things were happening behind his back that he didn't know about. Things he couldn't control. Ziggey started to sweat. What else might be going on? And where?

Now he couldn't decide whom to follow. Should he confront Patrick. Say he couldn't sleep and was driving around when he saw him? Should he see who those guys were?

His paranoia was festering. He saw weeks of planning, lying, and conniving going down the drain. His body started to shake with fear. There was a pinball careening inside his skull bouncing off what ifs. What would he tell Yoshi he did with all his money if he had to skip town? And skip town and the country is exactly what he would have to do. He could never return to New York, Greenwich Village or talk to his friends. Where could he go and how would he get there?

It was all unraveling, this was far too big a scam for him to carry off. Way beyond his ability. What ever made him think he could pull off something on such a grand scale? God just led him along, teased him until the final hour then wham! Stuck it to him. The old fool in the park was wrong. God was getting even for his years of crime.

"Wait a minute!" he said out loud as he watched Patrick's car exit the A&P parking lot and drive away. "You're overreacting. Calm down. Get hold of yourself. You're worrying about some snot nosed kid taking some pictures. Jerks like that are always taking pictures. They can't take a crap without a camera in their hands. You've seen guys like that all over the Village. Always have a camera with them. Shooting dogshit on the street, graffiti on the sidewalks and walls. Besides, have Robert question the little bastard later today. Whatever it was he could handle it. Enough already. Get some sleep." he thought.

Then he heard a car door slam behind him. He was relieved to see the three guys from the alley get into a parked police car. "So there, schmuck. What's to worry. Coupla cops out on a bender. Obviously they know the owner of the joint and probably were there all night drinking on the arm."

Ziggey decided to forgo his trip to Montauk and catch some sleep even if the damn dog woke the whole neighborhood. He'd just say he had to check on some locations for the day's shoot. No sweat. Nobody questioned the great producer.

He was exhausted, drained physically and mentally now, and would need to be well rested for Friday night.

There would be very little time for sleep from then on.

CHAPTER NINETEEN

Ziggey had calmed down considerably from the traumas of the night before, dismissing the events as   nervousness due to his impending wealth. He decided not to ask Robert to question Patrick. Why call attention to the unimportant. It had to be nothing more than this kid shooting stuff for himself probably to prove to his friends that he really did direct a movie in East Hampton.

What he didn't know, and wouldn't find out, is that Patrick had decided to make a documentary of his directorial debut. He had been shooting one to three hours of video tape a day ever since he arrived. He always had his mini cam with him and shot footage not only between scenes, but while he was directing had a production assistant use his mini cam to film shots of the film being made.

In addition, he videotaped every night, abjuring the parties and other social events, saying he had to work. He wanted to be ready for his interview on "Letterman" and "Entertainment Tonight."

Patrick savored the anticipation of viewing and then editing the start of his taped memories after work was finished on this film. This would serve to extend the incredible high he was on while waiting for the next assignment he was sure would come soon.

The next three days were spent shooting interiors. Ziggey was at every location taking an uncharacteristic interest. Again surprising Robert. "Why this sudden interest?" he thought, but didn't dare ask.

Ziggey would arrive early, before the crew showed up to assure the occupants of the care that would be accoreded their property and possessions. Then leave after getting confirmation that all their valuables were secured from potential damage or theft.

He would return later in the day, not concerned over the films progress, but to check and recheck the location of the valuables. He wanted to be able to navigate in total darkness if necessary. As anticipated, not only Ziggey, but everyone in the crew had total freedom in the house and on the grounds.

When shooting began in a particular house, ABZ security men were conspicuously positioned along the street and on the property. Ziggey had assured the local police that his personnel was more than up to the tasks of traffic control.

The Thursday night before the final day of filming, Ziggey had a late night meeting with his security people plus Robert and Patrick. Ostensibly the meeting was to discuss the logistics of the move to the next location, New York City, early Saturday morning.

Having worked out the planned departure, Ziggey said to Robert and Patrick, "I don't want to keep you guys. I know how much you got to do and everything. So, I'll settle up with these guys now since we won't be needing them in the city anyway. One less thing for you guys to worry about."

"OK. You're right. We do have a lot to do." Patrick answered relieved. "Got a lot of script to shoot tomorrow. I just hope we get it all done."

"I'm sure you will. You've done a great job so far." Ziggey said his arm around both their shoulders as he ushered them, pushed would be more accurate, to the door.

Robert had two thoughts. The first and most troubling was, "How the hell did he know we've done a great job? He never looked at any of the rough-cuts, and never asked if we

91

were on schedule, at least not until this week when we started interiors."

The other was, "Why were they being rushed out of this meeting? He felt something odd was going to go on in this room. But had no idea what.

This so-called security force neè: drivers had made Robert a little uncomfortable from the start. He didn't over hear film talk from them; gossip about other films they worked on, or gossip about actors or directors. None of the stuff the professional drivers talked about. They didn't have baseball jackets or hats with the names of other productions on them. He had never seen a movie crew that wasn't garbed in advertisements from their last or most famous picture.

Something wasn't Kosher. He'd try and figure it out when they got back to the city.

"OK, guys. Now let me tell you why you're here. Why I hired you." Ziggey started in a whisper after locking the door.

"Here's the skinny. I got something going that ain't got nothing to do with this fuckin' movie." The four men looked from one to each with knowing smiles. One saying, "I told these guys you had to have some hook into somethin'. I myself, never bought this movie crap to begin with." He continued with a smug "I told you so" look to the others. "Or that you all of sudden went straight. What you got goin'? Whatever it is, count me in long as I don't have to wear this fuckin' monkey suit anymore."

"Not so fast. You may not be so fuckin' anxious when I tell you what the deal is. But before I do, I gotta know who's in and who's out."

"How can we tell you that if we don't know what the hell you're doing?" another guy said.

"All I'm going to tell you now is that there's a ton of money to be made. And it's foolproof. I been working on this for a long time, got perfect plans and as you already figured out, plenty of dough behind me. Where the hell do you think I got the bread for this movie thing? This ain't from my salary in the joint."

"I need to know specifics." Said another.

"In or out? If you want out, you leave now." Ziggey said impatiently. "You say nothin' to nobody about nothin'. You takes your money and leave town by the first train in the morning. That's it. No hard feelings."

"Count me in." Three of them said in unison. The fourth man, after a brief pause said, "What the hell, this must be something real good for all the trouble you went to. Shit, what've I got to lose?"

"Nothin', You ain't got nothing to lose." Ziggey said. Then paused. "Except life if you fuck me over. I'm tellin' you, this is big. Bigger than anything you guys ever thought of, and I done all the work. You're comin' in at the end. The caboose on the gravy train."

Ziggey knew he could trust these guys from the old neighborhood. There was a code. Besides, once they knew his intentions and went along with him, no matter at what level, they would be guilty as accessories. Both before and after the fact. They also knew this.

He told them what he expected of them revealing only their individual tasks. There was no mention of Mr. Yoshi, Gary Gordon, Frankie the Fence, or his ultimate destination.

CHAPTER TWENTY

Filming was running late Friday. Not unusual in the movie business, but very upsetting to Ziggey. Patrick had mumbled to Ziggey about a bunch of audio problems that day.

"It started off with that damn helicopter pilot we hired for the aerial shots. He kept circling. That excited every dog in the neighborhood into fits of hysterical barking. I thought the audio guy could lose enough of it, make it ambient sound, but he told me no. We gotta re-shoot some stuff."

"When are you gonna finish?" Ziggey asked not at all interested in the specifics only the solution.

"I don't know for sure. The lighting will be difficult, we have to make it look like mid-afternoon and it's already starting to get dark. And the actors are tired. It's been a long day."

"Fuck the actors and the long day. With what those bastards get paid they should work twenty four hours a day and get it right the first time. Now tell me what time? I got to know. I got things to do."

"Should be outta here by six, seven the latest?"

"Six! You're done at six!" Ziggey said angrily as he walked away disgusted and worried.

Ziggey's plan would be much easier with empty streets, and ideal if the whole neighborhood was deserted as well. To serve that end, he had arranged a farewell thank-you party at the Laundry Restaurant.

A party to rival his arrival party. As before, the entire community was invited to this "Location Wrap Party."

The party was to start at six-thirty and last as long as the crowd wanted to stay. Ziggey needed exactly two hours to complete his operation.

Since Richard had little to do, he was put in charge of executing Ziggey's carefully choreographed serving plan for the party.

Ziggey would be there from six-thirty to seven as drinks were served. By then, Ziggey reasoned, everyone would have arrived. At seven, as appetizers were served, he would surreptitiously leave. If anyone asked for him Richard was to say he was making some business calls from his car, and would be back shortly.

He would arrive at his first destination at seven fifteen spending a maximum of fifteen minutes in each house. Some may only take ten minutes allowing travel time to the next location. This was not to be a hunt and search endeavor. He knew exactly where to go and what to do when he got there.

Food would continue to be served 'till nine. At nine-fifteen he would return to the party, as champagne was being served. He would offer a thank you toast and shake hands with as many people as time would allow.

Shooting did finish at six, as commanded, with Ziggey standing by. He told Patrick and Robert to take the crew and actors back to the cabins by cars to get ready for the party. He and his security men would see to the safe return of equipment and trucks.

Quickly, they loaded camera cases, lens cases, and large crates that held screens for lighting backdrops into two trucks. As soon as the first one was loaded it was driven to the vacant midway house on Georgica Road.

The Publisher owner was not coming out this weekend. Ziggey had called his office two weeks earlier on the subterfuge of wanting to interview him for a local newspaper and learned that he was to be at a sales conference in Los Angeles for the week.

Waiting at the house to help unload was another security man. When the truck was emptied and the contents brought into the large living room the driver returned to Ziggey while the security man emptied the cases of their contents of lenses, still and movie cameras, video recorders and audio equipment.

The emptied, aluminum cases were then lined up and left open on the living rooms two ten-foot sofas. The Styrofoam liners left intact.

By the time driver number one had returned to the house, the second truck had been loaded and was ready to pull out. He left his truck in front of the house and joined Ziggey and the two other men in this truck for the trip back to the midway house.

A similar procedure took place. Cases were quickly emptied and lined up in the living room. Ziggey then went to the party leaving three of his men at this house with one truck parked in the driveway. The fourth returned to guard the truck left at the first house.

Ziggey arrived, as planned, at the party at six thirty, giving him a half an hour to see and be seen. What he needed to see were the residents of the target houses. If those in town were at the party.

At seven he slipped out a side door of the restaurant hoping not to be seen leaving. A mixed blessing occurred; as he approached his car parked in the lot of the grocery store across the street, he was met by the husband and wife of the third house he was to hit on Lily Pond Lane. He was glad they arrived. Not seeing them inside caused him great concern. But why were they late? He wondered.

"Hey, glad to see you." Ziggey said shaking hands with both. "You're almost late. Nothing wrong at home I hope?"

"Not really just a disturbing surprise. A family matter. We'll survive. But it's good to see you too. You're not leaving already, are you?" They asked.

"No, no. Just have to make a few business calls from my car. See you inside soon. Enjoy."

Ziggey waited till they were out of sight before starting his car and leaving. "What the hell was a disturbing surprise to rich people?" He pondered while driving to his first location.

En route he made his first change of plans. Whatever it was disturbing these people might cause them to leave the party early. Maybe just have a drink to be sociable, to be seen so no one would think they weren't invited, and then leave. He better hit their place first, not third, as planned.

Ziggey punched out the computer code that gave access to the electronic gate protecting this property and drove to the side of the house. He looked around before entering, not as confident as he would have been had he not met this couple at the party and learned that they had disturbing news. He checked the garage to see if the right number and makes of cars that were supposed to be there were. Everything OK.

They had given him a set of keys when the crew filmed there as well as the combination to the outside gate. He had a duplicate set made.

Immediately he made his way to the basement game room replete with pinball machines, ping pong and bumper pool tables. Behind a picture on the wood paneled wall was a small safe. Hopefully they had taken his advice and put their valuables inside. While putting on his magnified eyeglasses to read the combination from his slip of paper, he heard a faint noise from somewhere in the house. Quickly checking the dossier for this house he saw there were no pets, nor live-in servants.

Maybe it was just his imagination or nerves playing with him, he thought, as he opened the safe. He wasn't disappointed with the contents. As expected there was the antique gold coin collection, several pieces of diamond jewelry, and many tightly banded bundles of cash.

"Wonder where the son of a bitch got all this cash?" Ziggey thought to himself. "Holier-than-thou bastards. Probably sells drugs on the side or something worse."

It wasn't money from drugs or anything as tawdry, (most of these people were above that sort of thing) but undeclared cash payments from a chain of fast food franchises that Yoshi had helped bank roll. This was not money that one could report stolen.

As he ascended the stairs he heard another noise, only this time it was louder, and clearly not his imagination. There was someone in the house. But who?

With his bounty in a black canvas satchel stenciled "Film Changing Bag" he quietly made his way up the stairs. It was quiet now. Whoever had been there, had seemingly left or was upstairs so he could leave unnoticed. But who had it been?

Just as he put his hand on the door knob, a male voice yelled, "Freeze or I'll blow your fucking head off!" Then he heard the distinctive click of a gun being cocked. The voice continued, "I'm not kidding. You wouldn't be the first burglar I've shot."

Ziggey, not anxious to reveal his face, remained facing the door.

"Hey, calm down. I ain't no burglar. Look," he said taking a set of keys from his pocket and holding them up and shaking them. "I got keys to the house. I don't know who you are, but you're making one hell of a mistake thinking that I'm a burglar. I didn't break in. You see any broken windows or anything? Did the alarm go off? Now put the gun down and I'll explain who I am and why I'm here."

Ziggey's logic prevailed pending further explanation. "OK, but it better be good. I'm an expert marksman." The voice answered with waning bravado.

When Ziggey turned and saw that the voice belonged to a teenage boy, he slowly approached him hand extended to shake. "Now put away that pea-shooter (it was a plastic BB pistol) and let me introduce myself and tell you what I'm doing here. And by the way, just who might you be and what are you doing here?" This was something that Ziggey had to know.

"I live here. This is my parents' house. I just came home from school to surprise them."

So this was the disturbing family business his parents spoke of in the parking lot.

"Oh, I get it. You were thrown out of school. What happened, they catch you with a chick in your room or something?" Ziggey said laughing. "Don't worry kid, I'm sure your old man can fix it. Now let me have that gun."

Still pointing this relatively harmless weapon at Ziggey the kid said, "You still haven't told me who the hell you are and what you're doing here?"

"Oh, right. I haven't have I?" Ziggey responded while looking at his watch. He had to get out of here and on to the next house. He was already five minutes behind schedule.

"Since you were away at school you probably didn't know about the movie company that's been in town for the last two weeks making a feature. I'm the executive producer, I'm surprised your parents didn't tell you. And what's even more interesting, we used your house, in the movie. Your folks gave me the keys, and the combination to the gate outside." Not waiting for an answer, Ziggey hurriedly went on, now moving to the door, anxious to finish his lie and get the hell out.

"Anyway, my stupid camera man left some undeveloped film downstairs, I got it here in this bag, and I got to get it to the lab right away. That's all there is to it." Looking at this watch again he opened the door saying as he left. "Good luck with school. See you in the movies."

"Shit! that was close." He said starting the car. "I gotta be more careful. Where did I screw up? I checked all the cars. His wasn't there. How'd he get home?"

99

CHAPTER TWENTY-ONE

The next house was uneventful. He had to try and put that damn kid out of his mind. Hope that it didn't matter. That the kid bought his story. Why wouldn't he buy it? It was perfectly logical, Ziggey kept telling himself.

Didn't matter anyway. There was no turning back now. Nevertheless, Ziggey was starting to sweat. Was this most careful of plans starting to unravel? These thoughts were tormenting him as he loaded the yield from this house into his car and drove to the next location.

Again, no problems, no surprises other than the delightful fact that the booty was bigger than anticipated. This guy must have hit the motherload after Yoshi went into the slammer. In addition to the stamp collection worth, perhaps, a million, and the cash, there were two small velvet bags containing God knows how many unmounted diamonds. He didn't stop to count.

This, Ziggey chose to view as reaffirmation that his plan was blessed. A good sign.

This finished his haul from the three Lily Pond Lane homes. Now to the three homes on the private road one of which was his residence of the last two weeks.

This was the safest of the venues for him. Nobody would be suspicious seeing him drive in or out of this road. Ziggey was exhilarated. He had accumulated more wealth in the last forty five minutes than in of all his prior criminal efforts put together. And he still had five houses to go. One of which held the ultimate prize. The one he had lived in.

The reason he was able to get the financing. The reason for Yoshi's interest.

Wall safes in both the master bedroom and den easily yielded their contents. And they were spectacular. He had to fight the temptation to spread the jewels out and assess them; count the cash; estimate the value of yet another gold coin collection; and total the bearer bonds. But fight it he did as he made his way to the paneled basement.

One wall of the paneled billiard room he entered at the foot of the stairs looked out on a sprawling lawn and the ocean. It worried him knowing that what he had to do could be seen from outside if someone should happen by.

It was dark now and he couldn't chance turning on even the smallest light. He had rehearsed the necessary movements many times during his stay here. Feeling his way to the pool cue rack on one of the walls, he fingered and counted the vertical sticks from the end of the rack. At number five of the ten there, he gently pulled the cue forward from its top clip and placed it on the floor. Then with a prayer, he turned the two prongs of the clip counter clockwise and held his breath while silently counting to ten.

"One thousand one, one thousand two, one thousand three." At ten he turned the clip clockwise back to its original position and waited the longest ten seconds of his life. Then it happened. The section of the wall housing the cue rack, thirty inches wide, moved silently backwards, stopped after a foot and then slid out of view to the right.

"I'll be a son of a bitch! It worked." Ziggey whispered as he moved into the cavity taking a small pen light from his pocket.

Barely two feet in front of him was a six foot high safe door the width of the this narrow corridor. Now for the last challenge. Had this combination been changed? He thought as he worked the numbers. Was all the information on Yoshi's disc unchanged? Success. "This is fucking unbelievable." He said out loud marveling in the technology and mechanics.   He caught himself mid-wonderment. "Come on! Get on with it! You'll have plenty of time to think about this later," he admonished himself as he entered a twenty-foot long room four times the width of the thirty inch entrance door. Leaving the safe door open, he slid past a two-inch thick steel door, closed it behind him, and turned on the room lights. The room was sealed, dust-proof, and temperature controlled.

Even though he was told what to expect, he had never been more astonished in his life. All three walls were hung with paintings by the Masters. Not that Ziggey recognized, nor could pronounce any of the artists names, but even he could tell this was expensive stuff. Just how expensive he had no idea.

Following Yoshi's orders he quickly removed two small Renoir oils (approximately ten by fourteen inches); two Monet oils, slightly larger, and two Van Gogh pencil sketches about the same size. All stolen art.

The Van Goghs were from the Rijks Museum in Amsterdam, missing for some forty years; the Renoirs from the Jeu de Paume' Museum in Paris; and the Monets from a private dealer in London. The dealer had never reported the theft so as not to frighten his clients.

This art had changed hands several times through a network of underground dealers who specialized in satisfying the egos of the world's highly competitive super rich. They would brag amongst themselves about purchases, one always trying to outdo the other.

The paintings safely hidden in a suit bag labeled "Wardrobe," Ziggey reversed his entry procedures, securing all the doors and making sure he returned the vault's door combination lock to the exact position he found it in.

The looting of the next two houses on the private road were uneventful, swift, and highly profitable, again yielding large sums of cash and jewelry.

Although tempting, Ziggey passed up fur coats, cameras, and anything else bulky. What he took, with the exception of the paintings, had to fit neatly into the waiting film equipment cases at the midway house on Georgica Road. His trunk loaded with booty, he drove off.

Stopping at the first house on Lily Pond Lane he ordered his security man there to take the truck he was supposedly guarding, and move it to block the street.

"Don't let nobody through till nine-thirty. You got it?" He told his man.

"Yeah, but what if someone gets pissed? What do I do then?"

"Like I told you before. Nobody is gonna show up. They're all at the party or out of town. Don't sweat it. But if anyone does show you do like I told you. You tell 'em, we got a crew working to remove very high voltage wires. It's dangerous. It's for their own protection. Then you give each a hundred bucks and tell 'em to go have drinks on ABZ. Our way of thanking them for any inconvenience we cause 'em."

"OK boss. But I sure hope nobody shows."

Ziggey was getting nervous about this guys resolve. He needed this time. By nine forty five he would be well on his way and didn't care.

"Just do like I told you. You wanta get your bread, or wind up in the slammer. Your ass is on the line same as mine, so do whatever you have to do, but nobody gets through!" He said driving off.

CHAPTER TWENTY-TWO

Having dropped off his bounty at the halfway house on Georgica Road, Ziggey was on his way to the final two targets on Quail Lane two blocks away. These two should be a piece of cake. They were next door to each other separated only by a four-foot high chain link fence, and one was owned by a movie star that he knew was in California making a TV series.

The folks from the second house were at the party.

He decided to hit the house of the people at the party first. This was a three-story gray shingled mansion set a hundred yards from the main road. Huge trees all but obscured the house from the road. Off the entrance driveway another road continued to a detached three car garage at the back of the house. Over this garage were former servants quarters that had been converted into lavish guest facilities.

As Ziggey drove down this side road, he was surprised to see a Mercedes convertible parked in front of the garages. Having checked the dossier on this house on his way over, he knew this car didn't belong.

He cut his engine and looked for signs of life. There were no lights on in the guest house so he guessed that it was a friend of the owners who went to the party with them. Not to worry. But he did worry as he checked his watch. Time was running short on his schedule. Maybe, he pondered, he should just pass on these two houses. After all, he had a ton of loot and the all important paintings for Yoshi. His obligation to Yoshi was satisfied and he could live a long time in South America on what he had stolen.

He waited another five minutes, and when he neither saw nor heard anything, greed took control of his decision. He had gone so far, it would be a pity to pass up these last two.

So decided, he entered the back door of the house with the duplicate of a key these people had given him so he might check out the inside at his convenience.

He also had a key to the back door of the actor's house next door. He got that from the actor's agent who also lived in East Hampton. Knowing his client's ego, the agent had almost pleaded with Ziggey to use his client's house for one of the interiors. When Ziggey demurred, saying that all the locations had been decided upon, he gave him a key anyway in the event he should change his mind. Ziggey graciously accepted the key, had a duplicate made and returned the original earlier this week with apologies.

So these two were to be easy. No complicated alarms or locks to deal with. The actor felt secure as his neighbors were full-time residents and they agreed to look after his property in his absence.

Once inside he moved quickly to the wall safe behind a Max Ernst painting prominently hung in the living room. This was easy as the couple had left lights on through out the house. Amazingly, the safe door was not locked. This caused him pause, was it empty? Had they cleaned it out for some reason? Not the case. Doing a quick inventory, as he loaded things into his camera bag, the only thing possibly missing was some ladies jewelry and a mans Rolex, probably being worn this evening.

In his anxiety to leave, he closed and locked the safe door, forgetting that he found it opened, and replaced the Ernst painting. A more sophisticated burglar would have ignored the safe's contents and just taken the painting, valued at several million dollars.

As he started over the four foot fence to the actors house he heard a noise. It sounded like a girl giggling. He stopped and listened. Another decision to be made. It was probably nothing to worry about. Could have come from a neighbor's house.

Should he go on or return to his car and get the hell out? Again greed made him go on. He was ahead of schedule now, so why blow this golden opportunity? Get all he could on this: his last chance for a huge score.

In this house he had to go to the master bedroom on the second floor for the safe. Using his small flashlight -- no luxury of house lights here -- he groped his way upstairs.

Wrong room. Then another wrong room. They were all so large it was confusing. Time was fleeting. Finally the right room, as his flashlight played across the seven-foot high armoire that served only as a false front for a safe.

Some years ago this bicoastal actor had sought Yoshi's fiscal advice after being ripped off by his California business manager. With no ulterior motive save their friendship, Yoshi suggested that he convert as much of his assets as possible into hard currency as a hedge against inflation; buy tax-exempt municipal bonds, and insist that his movie expense allowances be paid in cash. Further, in light of California's fires, mudslides, and earthquakes, he should buy a substantial safe and keep all the above in placid East Hampton.

Virtually the second after Yoshi's indictment, the actor turned on him. In a talk show interview, when asked about his neighbor and friend, he said he always thought this little Oriental was doing something not exactly kosher. He disavowed any friendship.

Access again was easy. This combination, as with the others, had not been changed since Yoshi was safely behind bars. When he got out there would be plenty of time to take care of that, so they all thought.

As Ziggey's hand touched the combination dial he exclaimed out loud, "Oh shit! I locked that damn safe next door." What the hell do I do now? he thought. Should I continue here or go back, unlock the safe and leave it open like I found it? His hands were starting to shake now. Why go back? What's the difference? They'll probably think they locked it anyway. Most likely, they'll come home drunk and just throw the jewelry on a bureau and won't go to the safe until morning when he'd be long gone.

On the other hand, maybe they left it opened deliberately? They would come home, throw the stuff inside and lock the safe without looking inside.

He looked out the window and checked his watch. He had some time, he decided, if he cut short his return visit to the party. Just grab the cash and any obvious gold pieces from this safe and get the hell out.

The whole operation took less than ten minutes. He would be OK as long as the neighbors didn't return early.

Back across the fence with his camera bag brimming, he was startled by a light in one of the windows over the garages. Immediately he hit the dirt and remained still. Barely breathing he stared at the window. Nothing. Then another light went on in a bathroom window and he saw the silhouettes of a man and a woman behind the frosted window.

One of them reached over and cranked open the window. As the window widened he heard the same giggle he had heard before. "They couldn't have seen me earlier," he thought, "or the place would be swarming with police by now."

Things threatened to unravel. His mind was racing with alternatives. "What the hell am I going to do now? I gotta go back into the house and unlock that Goddamn safe. With all the house lights on they could spot me. If I turn off the lights that may draw their attention. Then I gotta start the damn car."

107

He looked at his watch. Nine p.m.! He had fifteen minutes to be at the party. Then he heard the shower running. "Great! They'll be so busy with each other, they won't notice me or anything else for that matter," he thought, creeping forward slowly.

Just as he reached the bottom step to the door he heard a familiar man's voice from the garage area. He ducked behind the railing.

"Hey, it's beautiful out. Not a cloud in the sky. What'ya say we go for a walk on the beach? I have no intention of going to that stupid party anyway." The man said, leaning out the now wide open bathroom window.

"Jesus Christ! That son of a bitch!" Ziggey said under his breath, recognizing that it was Robert in the window. The face that joined Robert's for the view was the same broad he caught him diddling in the guest house last week. The one he forbid him to see.

"Damn, can't anyone do what they're told? I made that bastard more money in the last month than he's made in a year. He's supposed to be at the damn party covering for me. Well fuck 'em. I don't feel so bad about screwing him now." He muttered while checking his watch again.

Just then the window closed and Ziggey bolted up the steps and into the house, crawling along the floor to the living room safe. Leaving the safe as he originally found it, he crawled back out, and low to the ground made it to his car. The bathroom window light was out. He had to get out fast before the two emerged.

Putting the car in neutral, he pushed it out of the driveway to the street, jumped into the rolling car, started it, and sped to the halfway house.

Once there he and his security men emptied the car of its bagged booty and took it inside. He ordered the men outside to stand guard. It wasn't in Ziggey's interest to let them know exactly what he got or what he was about to do.

108

He then made three phone calls on his cellular phone, each programmed into the phones memory requiring only the push of one digit to complete the call.

The first: "This is Mr. Z. Be ready to take off at ten tonight." Click.

The second to "Frankie the Fence". "See you at nine forty five. Better have plenty or no deal." Click.

The third to Gary. "Arriving ten fifteen." Click.

While making the phone calls he arranged four piles of banded one hundred dollar bills on a glass coffee table estimating that each stack was worth three grand. From his pocket he took the pouch containing the unmounted diamonds and sprinkled about a dozen into an ashtray, returning the pouch to his pocket.

Then sorting quickly through various bags, he placed gold chains and bracelets, diamond and pearl earrings, Cartier, Tiffany, and Rolex watches, and assorted other small jewelry in an aluminum attaché-type camera case lined with Styrofoam.

The stamp, and coin collections, gold and silver bars, along with Bearer Bonds, T Bills, and big pieces of jewelry were placed in a larger aluminum case stenciled "long lenses."

Loaded and ready to go; attaché case, lens case, and wardrobe bag in hand he called his security men inside.

"There's your cut." He said pointing to the coffee table. "Should keep you guys happy and quiet. Lay low for a coupla of months, the shit's really gonna hit the fan, then get in touch with Frankie, he'll take care of them diamonds for you. Now I gotta get the hell outta here." Making his way to the door, he added, "Clean all this crap outta here." Pointing at the camera equipment and remaining cases, "I don't care what you do with it, just leave this place like we found it."

With everything secured in the trunk of his car he sped to the party hoping that all members of the looted houses would still be there.

It looked good, still lots of cars lining the surrounding streets. He had to be careful not to get blocked in a parking spot so he pulled in behind the closed grocery store across the street. As he got out of his car he heard a commotion. Men arguing, and then what sounded like a shot coming from inside the Deli.

"Shit! What now?" He thought, getting back in his car. "Better not park here. I don't know what's going on, and I sure as hell don't want to know." As he drove around to the side of the building, the glow from a street light was enough to illuminate a male figure running away.

As the man turned, apparently in fear of being followed, Ziggey first noticed that he was carrying a Video Cam and then the face. It was Patrick.

"Shit! What's with that little son of a bitch? What the hell is he doing?"

He waited silently in the car, nervously checking his watch. No more noise from inside. Patrick had disappeared amongst the cars in the parking lot of the Laundry restaurant. "Time to go," he said to himself.

CHAPTER TWENTY-THREE

Everything seemed OK at the party. Everyone was there. No sweat. Now to get out fast. He was behind schedule again. He had fifteen minutes to meet Frankie.

"Thanks so much for your most gracious hospitality." Ziggey repeated often as he hurried from person to person. "Hate to run, but gotta get to the next location. You know how it is. See you real soon again, I hope." And he was gone.

Back in the car driving west on Route 27 towards New York City, he kept checking his watch. It was nine forty. He had five minutes to the rendezvous. Just past a mini-mall he killed the car lights and turned onto a blacktop road off the highway. A barely discernible sign indicated by an arrow that this was the direction to the East Hampton Airport.

There were few houses in this area and no street lights. He didn't want his car to be seen driving to the airport.

As he approached the dark landing strip, Ziggey flicked headlights on and off three times then waited. Seconds later the signal was returned. He drove ahead to find Frankie waiting as pre-arranged.

"OK, let's do it." Frankie said impatiently. "What you got for me? I ain't used to this kinda arrangement. People come to me. This better be good."

"Stop runnin' your mouth and look for yourself." Ziggey replied as he opened his trunk and handed Frankie the aluminum attaché case.

"What's in here is all yours. Nice and neat." he said opening the case while he showed off the contents. "Hope you got enough bread with you to cover this."

"Very impressive, what you got here." Frankie said while examining the contents. He quickly sorted the watches into one section, and the gold chains and bracelets in another, appraising them as he did. He then spread out the jewelry examining each piece with a jewelers loop.

"Come on. Hurry up! How much you figure?" Ziggey asked impatiently, looking around nervously to see if he had been followed.

"Gimme a minute will you. You got some real good shit here."

"OK! OK! But hurry. I gotta get the hell outta here."

"Yeah, I know. Me too. Some of this shit ain't gonna be so easy to get rid of though. Got initials on 'em."

"Frankie, stop the shit. Stop tryin' to beat me outta a few bucks. You'll get rid of the initials the same way you always do, so cut the crap! It's me you're takin' to."

"Mr. Z, your plane is ready whenever you are."

"What! Who the fuck is he!" Frankie reeled yelling in terror, but also having the instinct to close the attaché case. "Where the fuck did you come from? What the hell is going on here Ziggey?"

"Calm down, Frankie. Finish what you're doin'." Ziggey said, taking the pilot by the arm and leading him out of earshot. "What the hell's the matter with you, you dumb son of a bitch, I told you I'd come to you when I was ready. What are you doin' here anyway? I ain't payin' you enough or somethin'?"

"No man. That ain't it. I just saw you and your friend over here and thought you might need some help."

"Thanks, but no thanks. I'm fine. Now get the fuck outta here. Where's the chopper anyway?"

"Like I told you. Behind the hanger. Over there." The pilot pointed as he left.

"What the fuck's the matter with you?" Frankie asked incredulous. "I told you, just you an me. Now I gotta reduce the price 'cause the risk just went way up."

"Listen, do whatever you gotta do! Just fuckin' do it so we can split." Ziggey said looking at his watch.

"Where you takin' the chopper to?" Frankie asked while counting out used hundreds and fifties.

"None of your fuckin' business. How much?"

"Well, I figure you got somewhere between a hundred and twenty-five to a hundred fifty grand." Frankie said hesitantly.

"Yeah, so what's it mean to me? Get on with it!"

"I'm bein' real generous with you 'cause we go back a long time..."

"Stop the bullshit, Frankie! How much?"

"As I told you, some of this stuff is gonna be hard to fence, even for a pro like me. I gotta do extra work, and that's gotta cost. So I figure, I'm bein' real good to you at ten cents on the dollar. Here count it out." He said handing Ziggey a stack of money. "Fifteen grand, all nice used bills."

"Frankie..." Ziggey said grabbing the money. "Go fuck yourself and fuck your extra work. I'm outta here you bastard."

Ziggey waited till Frankie drove off then got in his car drove behind the hanger, passed the chopper telling the pilot to start it up, and continued into the woods, hiding the car in a clump of trees and thick bushes.

He threw the bundle of Frankie's cash in the wardrobe bag where it mingled with the rest of the cash he'd stolen. With that and the aluminum lens case in hand, he boarded.

"You ain't seen nothing, or nobody! You got that straight, my friend?" Ziggey said menacingly.

"No sweat, Mr. Z. I'm the only deaf, dumb, blind pilot you'll ever meet. You got my bread?"

"Like I told you. You get it when you deposit me safely on the ground." Ziggey said as the chopper rose.

"OK with me. Fifteen minutes for ten grand's the most money I ever made in a day. Even for a night flight. By the way, how'd that aerial footage we shot of all those Osprey nests come out?"

"Great! It came out fuckin' great. Now get me to my next location without no more questions. OK?"

CHAPTER TWENTY-FOUR

As planned, Ziggey was deposited in a remote corner of Westchester County Airport, in Purchase, New York, in less than a half hour.

He paid the pilot and watched him take off. When the chopper disappeared over a hill, he walked into a wooded area of thick pine trees and hung the wardrobe bag from a low branch. Checking to see that he was safely hidden from view, he unzipped the bag. Reaching in, he fumbled through the stacks of cash at the bottom of the bag, feeling for, and finally extracting, a small canvas bag.

From this bag he pulled out a lady's shoulder-length wig, black with gray streaks, a plain black dress, black panty hose, sensible black heeled laced shoes, a black pocketbook, and a single strand of cheap pearls.

He changed into this outfit as quickly as he could manage with this unfamiliar attire. The panty hose covered his hairy legs. The long sleeved dress, his arms, and with the aid of pancake make up from a small compact, the hair on his face.

Ziggey, once the short bald strutting executive producer, was now a taller, homely "Little Old Italian Lady". Admiring this transformation in the compact mirror, he stuffed his clothes into the wardrobe bag and set off in the best womanly posture he could muster.

Arriving at the Avis car rental counter hc claimed the reservation for a two-door compact in the name of Mrs. Mangia presenting fake identification. So far so good. This was an area that had given him some concern even though he had rented cars before with forged ID. This time there was much more at stake.

Wardrobe bag, and lens case safely in sight on the next seat, he headed for the Tappan Zee Bridge that would take him across the Hudson River into New Jersey. He then planned to go south on the Garden State Parkway, to the New Jersey Turnpike and into Newark International Airport. At this time of night, barring accidents on the highway or car problems the trip shouldn't take more than forty-five minutes.

It went as scheduled, Ziggey listening to All News Radio for a "breaking story" regarding a burglary spree in East Hampton. No news. That didn't mean they hadn't discovered anything yet, just that the wire services hadn't heard of it.

He left the car at the Avis lot at Newark Airport using express check-in. He then boarded the Avis jitney that would take him to his midnight flight to Puerto Rico.

Once off the ground, he was giddy with success and had to fight off the temptation to remove his uncomfortable disguise.

"Not yet schmuck." He said to himself. "You still got two more legs of this trip. But, I did it! Dammed if I haven't pulled off the greatest scam of all time. I'll be famous. They're gonna make a movie of my life. I'll be more famous than Dillinger and I didn't kill nobody. I'll be one of them folk heroes."

The plane landed on schedule. He was on terra firma, out of the country. Let them try and find him now he thought.

"Hope the trip wasn't too trying for you?" Mrs. Mangia?" The stewardess at the door said. "You look a little pale."

Ziggey just nodded and made his way as quickly as possible down the stairs to the tarmac. Quickly as high heels

116

and dress would allow, he furtively made his way, as much in the darkness as possible to a small hanger on the back side of the airport. His charter plane was waiting to take him to Alice Town on the Island of Bimini.

Second leg over, he said to himself. Now for the final leg and a life of easy living.

"How are you, Mrs. Mangia?" Asked the pilot. Ziggey just nodded again. "Hope you had a pleasant flight. You're right on time," the pilot added, reaching for the wardrobe bag and lens case.

Ziggey pulled both parcels away and struggled into the small two-seater.

"Sorry, just trying to be helpful. Guess you must have some family heirlooms that you don't want out of your hands. Huh?"

Ziggey nodded in the affirmative thinking, "You don't know how right you are. Just not my family."

"We don't get many single lady senior citizens. Who'd you say you were visiting?" The pilot continued to make conversation as he taxied down the runway.

Ziggey made believe he was asleep clutching his possessions.

"Sorry again," said the pilot, "You must be exhausted from your trip. Well, I'll let you catch a nap then. It's a short flight." Then to himself. Hope someone is meeting the old bag. I don't want to get stuck with her one minute more than I have to.

Ziggey spent the flight concerned how he was going to get away from this too helpful pilot. He did not want to be helped to the terminal as he had no intention of going there. He planed to slip away unnoticed.

This was the only part of the plan that he had left to chance assuming it wouldn't be too hard. He would come up with something. He always did.

As the plane touched down in Bimini, the ever resourceful Ziggey had a plan. He took a pack of unfiltered Camel cigarettes from his pocketbook, lit one and took an obvious long drag.

"Hey put that out!" yelled the pilot. "Want get us killed?"

Ziggey immediately took another drag, then while bending over to stamp out the butt he started to cough. The deep rasping cough of a three pack a day smoker. He continued to cough making his whole body tremble as they taxied to the terminal building.

The pilot, in his anxiety, couldn't wait to get away from this disagreeable passenger, couldn't cut the engines fast enough. He jumped out and ran to the passenger side opening the door and lowering the built in steps as fast as he could offering his hand to help.

Ziggey, while waving off the offer of help with his right hand, grabbed his throat with his left hand and forced himself to throw up inside the cockpit.

That act sealed his solo departure. This was the final straw for the disgusted pilot.

"Listen lady, can you make it to the terminal by yourself. I gotta clean this up right away. I got a five a.m. flight with some very fancy people and..."

Ziggey deplaned, more deftly than he should have, and disappeared into the darkness.

CHAPTER TWENTY-FIVE

About the time Ziggey boarded his flight to Puerto Rico people started to leave the party and return home. Most people didn't immediately discover the illegal entry to their homes or their loses. They simply came home watched the late news and went to bed. The only reason to go to a safe was to return something taken out for the evening which only one couple had done.

The couple on Quail Lane that Ziggey thought had deliberately left their safe open. Not the case. A hell of a domestic battle ensued. "Hey! The damn safe is open." The husband said returning his twenty thousand dollar Rolex. "You told me you were going to close it." The wife replied from another room. "Bullshit!" Yelled the husband. "You said you were going to get your diamond earrings." He said starting an inventory.

"I changed my mind. What's the big deal anyway? You and that stupid safe. I don't know what we need it for anyway."

"Jesus Christ!" Screamed the husband. "You stupid bitch! I've been cleaned out!"

"What're you talking about?" Cleaned out? Cleaned out of what?" The exasperated wife said, entering the room. "I don't know what you're so worried about. That's why we have insurance. Besides, I was tired of some of that stuff anyway."

"You don't get it, do you? I had over a hundred thousand dollars in cash stashed here. It's all gone. And it sure as hell isn't covered by any insurance policy."

"What? I don't understand? Where did you get that much cash?" She asked shocked.

"None of your business. You don't want to know. I gotta call Al. See if they got hit."

"Why should Al and Dawn also be robbed? You aren't involved in anything illegal are you?"

He didn't answer her as he punched out the phone number.

After Al checked his safe their worst fears were realized. Over a quarter of a million in cash stolen and they could do nothing about it. Screw their wives' jewelry.

Word spread quickly as more phone calls were made with the same results. It soon became clear that this was a well thought out series of burglaries. But who?

Then it hit them. They were all at the movie company's party when it happened. First thing in the morning they would check on the credibility of the movie company and that Ziggey fellow.

By midnight East Hampton, from Georgica Beach to Main Beach, was ablaze with lights.

There were cops all over. Off duty cops were called out of bed. The FBI office in Riverhead, the County Seat, an hour's drive away, was notified as well as the Coast Guard station at Montauk Point. Back-up police from South Hampton, Bridgehampton, and Sag Harbor were called in. Highway Twenty-Seven was closed in both directions blocked by heavily armed police. No one was permitted in or out of East Hampton. The prevailing wisdom was that the thieves must still be in the area judging by the sheer amount reported stolen.

Then people started remembering things under questioning. "Anyone suspicious around before you went to the party?"

"No, nobody but some guys from the movie company." The standard response.

A quick conference by the authorities sent six screaming patrol cars to the Cozy Cabins. They surrounded the entire compound and called in a firetruck to illuminate the area.

Everyone was unceremoniously rousted from their beds and hauled outside while their rooms and vehicles were searched. Torn apart would more accurately describe the actions against these outsiders.

Neither Richard, Robert nor Patrick were in their rooms. It was quickly assumed by the head detective on the scene that those three along with that phony Executive Producer were the culprits.

"I never trusted those slimy bastards." Said one of the cops. God damn movie people. Too slick for my taste." As he said this Richard drove up.

"Hey, what the hell is going on here?" He yelled as he was pulled roughly from his car by two cops.

"Like you don't know? Wise guy." One said.

"I don't know! What is this?" He repeated incredulous.

"Where's the goods, and where are your partners?" A detective asked while Richard was being handcuffed.

"I don't know what the hell you're talking about. What goods?"

"Where's that so-called producer guy, Robert what's-his-name, and that little bald headed son of a bitch? Oh, yeah, and that long haired kid you called a director? We got you so you might as well cooperate."

"You're all nuts." Richard said. "This must be a bad dream. I have no idea what you're talking about? And I don't know where anyone is. I assume Robert and Patrick are here. I haven't seen them all evening. I've been at the party since five o'clock. Mr. Z wasn't staying with us. Some fancy house near the pond. That's all I know."

"Take him downtown and book him for burglary. We'll sweat it out of him later," ordered the detective to a uniformed officer.

As the patrol car left with Richard handcuffed in the back seat, Robert pulled in recognizing Richard. He immediately started a U-turn to follow the police car to find out what was going on, but was thwarted when the detective yelled to a cop at the entrance to "stop that car." He did this by ramming Robert's car.

Robert was treated the same as Richard while protesting his ignorance of anything untoward.

"Where you been? We know you wasn't at the party. Why don't you just confess now? Make it easy on yourself. Turn in your scumbag friends and maybe we can make a deal. I'll recommend they go light on you." the detective implored.

"I don't know what you're talking about."

"OK, fine. Book him. Maybe when the two of them get together in the slammer they'll smarten up."

While this was going on at the motel, another team of detectives was questioning the home owners. The first on Quail Lane.

"When did you discover you'd been robbed?"

"When I went to my wall safe to put my watch away and found the damn thing open."

"What was stolen? I assume you have an inventory list?"

"Yeah, of course. Not too much though. Guess we were lucky. Just some of my wife's jewelry. Not serious. We're insured." His wife started to say something, but her husband's glare shut her mouth.

"Did either of you see anyone hanging around, anyone that might have looked suspicious in the neighborhood?"

122

"No. Not really. Just those nice folks from the movie company." She added.

"I'm afraid they're not so nice. We have every reason to believe that they're the ones who broke into everyone's home."

"Really? I find that hard to believe." Offered the wife. "They seemed like such nice people. Particularly the Producer, Robert. What a gentleman. I can't believe that he would be mixed up in anything illegal. We got to know him quite well, you know?"

"No, I don't. Why don't you tell me what you know about him." Asked the detective.

"Well, not that much actually." She answered warily now. "He spent a lot of time with Tiffany in our guest house."

"Tiffany? Who's Tiffany?"

"Tiffany Cohen. Her folks live over on Lily Pond. Anyway, she just graduated from college and didn't want to move back in with her parents so we told her she could live in our guest house by the pool. It's really quite lovely. Would you like to see it?"

"Not now. Thank you. But I will want to check it out later. You said this Robert spent a lot of time with Tiffany in your guest house?"

"Yes, they make a beautiful couple. I think they may even get married."

"Did you see either one of them at the party?"

"Well, actually, no, now that you mention it. Did you see them dear?"

"No I didn't. What the hell's the difference anyway? It's too late. They're probably long gone by now. If you don't mind detective, I'm going downstairs for a night cap. Would you like a something from the bar?"

"No thanks. This is going to be a long night. OK, I think I have everything I need for now." The detective said closing his notebook. "So if you don't mind, I'd like to check out your guest house. I figure this Robert was just using your friend Tiffany. He might have left something in her house figuring no one would ever look there. Do you know if she's home? The place looks dark."

"I don't know, but I'm sure she's asleep. Let me call first so we don't scare her."

The awakened Tiffany was appalled by the detective's assertions that her Robert would be involved in anything even remotely criminal.

"Where you with Robert tonight?" The detective asked, ignoring her pleas of innocence. He'd heard all that stuff before.

"Yes, yes I was. So what?"

"Where were you? We know you weren't at the party like everyone else."

"We stayed here. Right here. We had a candlelit goodbye dinner by the fireplace."

"Did you stay in all night or go out after dinner?"

Annoyed with the allegations she tersely replied, "Yes we did go out. We went for a long walk on the beach. Is that a crime?"

"Anyone see you? Anyone who can verify that?"

"I don't like your tone of voice or what you're implying. But, no, no one saw us. Will that be all?"

Unmoved by her attitude he continued. "Did you see or hear anything suspicious while you were home? Anything at all, like a car or truck, maybe in the driveway?"

"No," Then thinking a minute. "Well, I thought I heard something. It could have been a car door."

"Did you check it out?"

"No. We were kinda busy at the time and besides Robert said he didn't hear anything, it must have been my imagination."

"Uh huh. That's exactly what he wanted you to think. You know what I think young lady? I think your friend was using you. He was here as a lookout."

"Where is he?" she asked now concerned that she, in fact, might have been used. "I want to see him."

"I was just informed on the way over here that he is where he belongs. In jail!"

CHAPTER TWENTY-SIX

Out of sight, in the darkness at the end of a runway, next to the water, Ziggey made his final wardrobe change. This one not quite so radical. A toupee, false mustache, (this just until he raised his own), and lifts for his shoes.

Placing the ladies clothes and accessories back in the small canvas bag along with his black Producer duds he added the heaviest stones he could find and deep-sixed the package.

Now the slightly taller, more colorfully dressed Ziggey looked like just another island tourist as he registered as Ralph Wilson at a small motel near the airport. One that had seen better days.

Paying in advance for a week's stay he went to his room and even though it was four a.m. sleep was impossible. Ziggey was euphoric.

"I did it! God damn if I didn't pull off the greatest scam of all time. I can't wait to see just how great," he kept repeating as he paced around the room. He knew he'd done well, but now was the moment of truth. What he'd been looking forward to all evening. Just how well?

First to make sure the room was as secured as it could be. He locked the windows, closed the blinds and then the shutters behind them. After moving a dresser in front of the door, he went into the bathroom, wardrobe bag in hand, and locked the door behind him.

Unzipping the bag upside down he let the contents spill into the bathtub while holding onto the paintings inside. It was a wonderful sight. Hundreds and hundreds of banded stacks of large bills covering the entire bottom of the tub.

It was dawn by the time he finished the best job he ever had in his life, counting some four hundred thousand dollars of his money.

"The perfect crime. Ain't nobody gonna report stuff stolen they already stole. And I did it! Me, short little Ziggey Zignorelli from Brooklyn. A nobody. Well, now I'm a somebody! It's great! And this ain't all of it. The best is yet to come." He said, running his fingers lovingly through the stacks of cash as he replaced it neatly in the bag and returned to the bedroom.

"Now just exactly what've we got here?" He said opening the lens case. It was beautiful to see as he sorted some of the things on the bed, but he had no idea what, coins, stamps and the bearer bonds would yield him. The jewelry he figured would get only ten cents on the dollar, but he had no idea of the worth. Didn't matter. Four hundred thousand tax free bucks would last him a hell of a long time.

At six a.m. he went outside with his cellular phone and punched in a pre recorded number.

"I'm here. Where?" Was all he said. Then listened to brief instructions saying nothing in response and hung up.

"OK. That's easy. Now one more detail." He went back into the bathroom tearing a sheet out of a phone book on the way. He crumbled the page putting it in the sink. Then opened his wallet and removed his coded dossiers sheets placing them on the paper lighting the pile with a gold Dunhill lighter he'd stolen. When the fire went out, he soaked the ashes and flushed them down the drain.

"Done. It's gonna be a great life from here on out." He said relaxing on the bed next to his booty.

"That son of a bitch better show." He said, looking at his recently acquired Rolex.

At exactly six thirty there was a faint knock on the door. Three taps, pause, then two, pause, then one.

"Who?" Ziggey asked leaning over the dresser.

"G and A pick up service." The whispered response.

"OK, just a minute." Ziggey answered while sliding the dresser aside and unlocking the door. "Come on in. The stuff is ready." The contrived dialogue in case someone from another room or a maid should over hear.

"Wow! You sure pulled it off." Gary exclaimed as he rushed to the bed covered with a fence's dream.

"Heard anything on the news?" Ziggey asked.

"No. Not a word. You really must have them baffled."

"Nothing, not one mention of the greatest scam of all time?" Ziggey asked, disappointed with the lack of notoriety.

"Hey man, what're you worried about? Thought you'd be happy." Gary said while fingering and appraising the loot.

"Well, sure...but I thought..."

"Thought what? Be happy, man. You're home free." Gary said removing a small calculator from his gaudy sports-jacket pocket.

Ziggey sat in a chair and watched as Gary figured on the calculator and made notes on a small pad. "Good stuff. You got some real good stuff here. No sweat getting rid of the stamp and coin collections. Just a matter of who I choose to sell 'em to. Jewelry also a piece of cake. Probably will break some of the stones out of their settings. That way no one can identify the pieces. Get more bread that way." He made some more notes then ran a total and handed the page to Ziggey. "Here's what I figure, so far, not counting the bonds. How's that grab you?"

"Fine. Looks good to me. I assume you have the cash with you?" Ziggey responded without enthusiasm.

"Of course, my good man. Cash and Carry Gary they call me. Hey, be happy man. You did great. What the hell are you so down about? You don't want publicity. Believe me, by now they're working to keep it from the media. Those rich people have power. Besides you embarrassed the shit out of them. It may never make the news. My stuff never does. It's the best thing that could happen to you. Cheer up."

That was not what Ziggey wanted to hear even though Gary was right.

Figuring some more as he leafed through the bonds, Gary's eye caught the wardrobe bag resting on a chair in the corner of the room.

"Ok, my friend, I'm done with this stuff. What's in that bag over there?"

"A present." Ziggey answered matter-of-factly.

"A present. That's nice. What is it, if you don't mind me asking?"

"I do mind. It's none of your fucking business. Now are we through here? If so, pay me and get the hell out. I'm tired."

"Hey, sorry. Don't be so touchy. I just thought that it might be some more stuff that you forgot to show me. I was just trying to be helpful. Looks like it might be a painting or something?" Gary suggested noticing the outline of a frame hoping this observation would elicit an answer.

Gary was more than just curious. He wanted to know. Bounty such as this didn't come that often and if what was in the bag was from one of those houses, he assumed it had to be of great value. If it was, in fact, paintings they were probably worth more than this dumb punk would know anyway. He could really screw him on this one.

"What's it to ya? Like I told you, it's a gift for a friend. No big deal." Ziggey said getting up and going to the bathroom.

"I'm just trying to be helpful. Like I said. That's all." Gary said as Ziggey closed the door behind him, then quietly headed for the bag. He had to know. It was killing him thinking that Ziggey might be holding out something really great. He hadn't bought that gift for a friend stuff for a minute. Coughing as he slid the zipper open, he quickly appraised the contents and closed the bag. So much for honor among thieves.

"Son of a bitch!" He exclaimed under his breath. "How'd that little bastard come by this?"

"Listen." Ziggey said, coming out of the bathroom. "It was nice doin' business with you, but I gotta go." He said looking at his watch heading for and picking up the wardrobe bag. "I got an appointment."

"So that's it. The bastard has a deal for those paintings. I'm getting cut out of the score of a lifetime." He thought.

"I can't let you do it." Gary said, blocking the doorway with his body.

"Can't let me do what?" Ziggey said, trying to push him aside.

"Do you have any idea what you have in that bag?"

"Yeah, I told you. A present for a friend. What's it to you? Get the fuck outta my way, or I'll deck ya."

Not feeling threatened by the much smaller man, Gary didn't yield his position. "Do you have any idea what those paintings are worth? I looked when you were in the can. Sue me."

"Yeah, so what. A lot of money, I figure. Maybe five, or ten grand each. Maybe more? They look expensive."

"Five or ten grand? How about five or ten million each, you dumb bastard. That's some present. Level with me. You got another fence. Right? Gonna cut me outta this. Right?"

"No." Ziggey said taken aback by this recent bit of intelligence. "You sure? You know what you're talking about? Five or ten million each? You gotta be shittin' me?"

"Let's talk a minute." Gary said, taking the pondering Ziggey by the shoulder leading him to a chair. "Your friend or whatever, can wait. Sit down and I'll impart some cultural wisdom.

"What you got here are paintings by some of the worlds most famous artists. I deal in a lot of art so I know what I'm talking about. I can't speak for the Van Gogh drawings, but I recognized the Renoirs and Monets. They've been missing since World War Two. Given up for lost. Most experts figure they were stolen by the Nazis' and either destroyed in the bombing of Berlin or that some German family still has them hidden.

"To give you an idea, an exceptional Renoir just sold for twenty five million at an auction in New York. These could be worth half that."

Gary had his attention. His mind racing with numbers beyond his comprehension. That and his promise to Yoshi. All Yoshi had told him was that the paintings were valuable and that they were stolen. Not that they were worth millions. He shoulda told him. Maybe he could have taken more?

"You listening?" Gary asked the distracted Ziggey.

"Yeah. But I got a problem. I owe this guy. Owe him big time. We had a deal. My part was to get him these."

"Fuck him. Where did you get these anyway? They sure as hell weren't hanging in someone's living room in East Hampton I can tell you that for sure."

"Locked in a vault in a guy's house."

"Fine. What we got here then is what I thought. Stolen art. Nobody can do anything about it."

"So what can you do?" Ziggey asked.

"I sell this kind of stuff all the time. Big demands among those Hollywood assholes always trying to one up one another. Granted I never had anything this big, but believe me when I tell you, I can get rid of them. I'm the man for the job. Probably the only guy in the world that can pull this kind of deal off. Trust me."

"He'll kill me." Ziggey said half out loud.

131

"Who'll kill you?" Gary said elated. He'd won. "First he'll have to find you. And with the kinda money we're gonna have you can buy a country and army to go with it. What're you worried about, partner?"

CHAPTER TWENTY-SEVEN

"Where's that snot-nosed, make believe director?" The chief of detectives asked Robert and Richard in an interrogation room.

"I have no idea. The last I saw of him he was shooting at a house on Lily Pond Lane. I don't know where he is. I'm not his keeper." Robert answered, annoyed as hell at being in this situation.

"No, but you're his boss, schmuck. Where is he? Take off with the loot?"

"I told you I don't know."

"Wasn't he at the party?"

"I wasn't there. Did you see him?" Robert asked the visibly shaken Richard.

"No." he answered. "Listen what is all this about? Why are we here? What loot are you talking about anyway?" Richard asked the detective.

"As if you didn't know. Wise guy. Damn near every house south of the highway has been burglarized."

"What's that got to do with us?" Robert interjected. "So you got an active burglar in town who took advantage of people being at a party."

"You got that right, college boy. And you're the guys that did the taking advantage. Soon as I get a report back from the FBI on your sleazy boss, I'll have all the proof I need. I don't suppose you'd like to tell me where he is either?"

"Don't know." Richard said. "He wasn't staying with us."

"Doesn't matter. We should have him in custody soon. He was at the party around nine thirty so he couldn't have gotten very far. We got the whole island sealed off, airports, bus terminals, train stations and roadblocks set up all the way to the God damn Midtown Tunnel. He's ours."

Meanwhile Robert's mind was racing. His concerns of the past were starting to fall in place. Ziggey's lack of attention. His shaved head. The goons he hired as drivers. This cop probably had something. And what about Patrick? Where the hell was he? Was he involved with Ziggey? Didn't make sense. A nice kid like that.

The detective was called out of the room.

"Ah, good." said the cop. "That's probably the fax I'm waiting for from Washington. Just relax boys and think real hard about cooperating. Might be able to save you a few years in the slammer."

This was the first time since they were arrested that Richard and Robert were left alone.

"What the hell is going on here?" Richard asked, visibly shaken.

"I'm not exactly sure." Robert answered. "But it looks like we've been set up as the biggest patsies of all time."

"What'd you mean, 'set up?'"

"Looks like our good friend and neighbor used us to make a phony movie so he could loot the town."

"You're kidding. Why? The movie seemed legitimate enough to me. Hell, look at the money he spent."

"Exactly. Look at it. Where did it really come from? And who the hell is this mysterious backer of his? Why did we pay for everything in cash? You ever work on a movie and get cash? Ever see Ziggey at the viewing of the day's rough cut film?"

"Well no," Richard answered not liking what he was hearing. "Why didn't you say anything to me if you were so suspicious?"

"Simple, I didn't want to believe it. I thought this might be my big break, or even a small one. I wanted to believe that we were on our way, both of us, to some success. That son of a bitch. I hope they catch him."

"What about us? They think we're involved." Richard's head was swimming with fear.

"I don't know. Somehow we're gonna have to convince them that we're innocent. That we were duped the same way everyone else was."

"Maybe when they catch him, he'll do the decent thing and let us off the hook. Who knows?"

"I can't believe Patrick had anything to do with this?" Richard went on.

"Me either. And that's another thing that bothered me, why hire someone with no experience?"

"Well you know, I was against him from the beginning. Made no sense to hire a novice. You talked me into him."

"I know. Sorry about that. I got sucked in by my own ambitions. Ziggey obviously figured he could buy us with money and the dream he knows we have. The same with the kid. And the kid wouldn't ask any questions, at least not of Ziggey. He gave us the job of lying for him. Wonder how much he got and where the little bastard is?"

The sun was about to rise, as everyone connected with the movie was herded into the station house. A crowd of outraged citizens had already assembled outside ready to lynch the whole crew. They were angry and at the same time embarrassed by their trusting naivety. Word spreads very quickly in a small town, and this community of so-called sophisticates was no exception.

Some were not so anxious that Ziggey be caught. They just as soon he got away. Far away. None could lay claim to

135

the cash, or admit that they had anything stolen. The IRS was sure to hear of this case. So they just had to bite the bullet and lie as best they could to their insurance brokers.

After exhorting her father to use his considerable influence, Tiffany got in to see Robert. They could have five minutes alone.

"OK. What's the story?" Asked a very upset Tiffany.

"Short and simple. We were screwed by Ziggey. The movie was a scam, and unless we can prove differently, we're all gonna be indicted as co-conspirators. None of us had anything to do with it. Well, that may not be true. Maybe some of his goon friends were in on it. But certainly not Richard, Patrick, the actors, or me."

"That's it?"

"No. One more thing. I love you."

"I believe you."

"Which? That I'm innocent or that I love you?"

"Both. I'll have daddy get right on this. Don't worry." She kissed him as she got up to leave.

"I am worried. What makes you think a hotshot lawyer like your father will represent me? Besides, I can't come close to paying the kinda fees he gets."

"I told you not to worry. He'll do it. Trust me."

CHAPTER TWENTY EIGHT

Gary left Ziggey, confident that they had established a partnership for the sale of the paintings. The ever-crafty Ziggey still wasn't so sure. But this recent revelation made for an interesting option. For now, let Gary think what he wants. After all I still have the paintings in my hands, he reasoned.

Gary left the island with his lens case of acquisitions. How he left or where he was going did not concern Ziggey. Nor was he told. Only that he would return in five or six days with a buyer for the paintings, admonishing Ziggey to make sure they were secured.

Ziggey had an appointment he'd made before Gary showed up. An appointment he now wasn't sure he would keep. The call to Mrs. Yoshi had established that he had escaped with the paintings and was where he said he would be. Her brief instructions simply conveyed the name of a bank and a banker. He knew what to do. She would inform Yoshi.

Ziggey's hedge was simple, if Gary showed up, which was by no means guaranteed, and he had a buyer he would go along with Gary. He would have time to get the paintings back from the bank on some subterfuge. As near as he could remember, Yoshi still had about six months to serve on his sentence. Better for now to let Yoshi know that the deal they made in prison had been honored. That his investment in Ziggey paid off.

If Gary didn't show, Yoshi wouldn't be any the wiser and he could have his paintings. Granted the prospect of millions was enticing, but Ziggey knew what he didn't know. This was way out of his league. And he had the sense to know it. So, Ziggey as Ralph Wilson, went to the bank and made his deposit in the vault.

Feeling a little letdown after the exhilaration of the past two weeks, it was now time to start enjoying the fruits of his work. Start a life he'd only heard about and seen in movies.

He checked into a suite in the most luxurious hotel on the Island, ordered a lavish breakfast from room service, hung out the Do Not Disturb sign, and after breakfast slept the entire day.

It didn't take Ziggey long to sample all that the good life had to offer. He was the hit of the hotels guests and staff, buying drinks at the bar, throwing parties in his suite, and tipping lavishly. He had the proverbial wine, women, and song that he had coveted for so long.

This was where he would live, he decided, not in this hotel, but ultimately find a house in a quiet setting by the beach, returning to the hotel only when he felt a need for night life. Of course, he had given no thought to what he would do all day. Ziggey was not a man with hobbies or interests other than running scams, interrupted only briefly by eating and drinking. Life would be great from here on out he was convinced.

CHAPTER TWENTY-NINE

Things were not going well for Richard and Robert. On their second day in jail, a Grand Jury was convened. An indictment seemed certain within twenty four hours. The community was so convinced of their complicity, even though they knew, by now, that Ziggey had escaped with the loot, that even Tiffany's father could not get them out on bail. The judge said it was as much for their own protection as it was for the courts.

There were no leads on Ziggey's or Patrick's whereabouts. They both seemed to have disappeared into thin air. Little did they know. All law enforcement was now convinced that the kid was his partner. Even the cops were impressed with the clean getaway. The helicopter never occurred to anyone. Ziggey's black Mercedes still hadn't been found, and no one had seen him drive to the airport. Beautiful.

So, with Ziggey gone, they had to hang this most embarrassing of crimes on someone. At least they had these two, was the prevailing wisdom.

The media had a field day. There were now legitimate camera crews and reporters all over East Hampton. Most of the robbery victims refused to be interviewed as the press wasn't treating these duped folks very kindly. What now seemed like obvious questions; "Didn't you confirm the credibility of the movie company before opening up your community to them?" "Didn't anyone have the intelligence, or at least the curiosity, to run a simple credit check?"

"How could these highly educated, sophisticated, people be so naive?" was a frequent lead line. Another paper led with. "East Hampton is now famous as the brunt of the Great Movie Robbery."

"I wonder what the hell happened to Patrick?" Richard asked Robert in the cell they shared.

"Beats the hell out of me. I hope he's OK though. I'm still convinced he had nothing to do with this." Robert said.

"I'm not so sure anymore. I mean if he's innocent where is he? He's obviously in hiding or the cops would have found him by now. Doesn't look good to me. I think he's involved someway." Richard said.

"Hope not." Robert said more concerned about his own life now. "I still like the kid."

As if his ears were ringing, Patrick showed up at the Cozy Cabins while that very conversation was taking place. He drove in as nonchalantly as any tourist and headed for his former cabin.

Police surveillance had been withdrawn the day before after a thorough search of every room. At this point everyone was suspect, and the cops weren't so sure that the owner might not have had some part in this.

Patrick still had his room key so entry was easy.

"Jesus Christ! What the hell happened here?" He said entering the room and stumbling over some drawers the police had left on the floor. He, of course, knew from the media that everyone had been arrested, had even seen shots of the motel on television.

"Guess it's pretty dumb of me, expecting to find any of my equipment or notes." He said out loud.

"Dumb ain't the word for it kid!"

"What! Who the hell are you?" Patrick said, turning to see a very large and very menacing man blocking the doorway, pointing an even more menacing pistol at him.

"I'm your keeper, dummy. Now shut up and get face down on the floor or I'll have to put you there, and you could get hurt in the process."

"OK, but I don't understand," doing as he was told.

"Fine, I'll explain it to you then. You got the right to remain silent, an attorney, etc., etc., etc.

"Meanwhile you're under arrest." The cop said while clasping handcuffs on the prone Patrick.

"You mind telling me what for? I haven't broken any laws."

"We got a list a mile long starting with Grand Larceny and unlawful flight, we even got you now for breaking and entering; this room is off-limits to everyone but police. Get up, I got some people who'll be real happy to see you."

As they drove by the owner's cabin on the way out of the compound, the cop stopped and yelled. "Thanks for the call Roy, you did good. I'll be sure and tell the chief."

As the door to the cell area was opened, Patrick was still protesting his arrest.

"Hey, Richard." Robert said. "Doesn't that sound like Patrick's voice?"

Before he could answer, Patrick was led past their cells to an adjoining one.

"What're you doing here? I thought you got away?"

Richard blurted out. The arresting officer heard this outburst as an incriminating statement.

"Gottcha now, sonny." Laughed the cop.

"Jeeze, I didn't mean it that way." Richard tried in vain to explain.

"OK, this should wrap things up pretty quickly now that we got three out of four." The cop said, locking the cell door. "Your buddies in crime here have been pretty stubborn, not to mention stupid, but I'm sure a smart kid like you will want to cooperate. It would go well with a judge if you blow the whistle on the shithead Producer. We're gonna get him

141

anyway. So you might as well make it easier for yourself. One of the other detectives will come for you soon. So think about what I just said."

"Thank you officer. I'll think about it." Patrick said to the officers back, winking at Richard and Robert with a wry smile on his face.

After the cop closed the door behind him Richard uncharacteristically grabbed Patrick through the cell bars. "What's so damn funny? Don't you know what's happened, what's going on? We're in deep trouble here. They want to hang us."

Robert had a sense that something good was going to happen. Richard was overreacting. Patrick had to know what was going on. He was far from stupid. He came back for a reason and he felt the reason had something to do with their freedom.

Arms folded across his chest with a smile on his face Robert said, "Richard, let go of him. Let him speak. I get the feeling we might be in for the best news we've had in days?"

"Yeah, Richard let go." Patrick said. "I gotta talk fast before they come for me. Robert come closer, we gotta be careful. Bottom line is we're home free. Should be outta here by tonight?"

"But how? Why?" Richard whispered. "You tell 'em where Ziggey is or something?"

"No, I haven't told them anything. And I don't know where Ziggey is, or care for that matter, but I got chapter and verse on him. It's gonna buy us all complete vindication."

Just then the door to the cell room opened, a detective entered and took Patrick to the interrogation room.

"What the hell is he talking about?" Richard asked.

"I have no idea." Robert said, "But I have every confidence in him. Don't you get it, Richard? He came back to get us out and clear his name. He didn't have to

142

come back. He got himself arrested deliberately. I told you he was a good guy. I think I'm starting to enjoy this now?"

Fifteen minutes into the questioning of Patrick by the head of detectives, they were interrupted by a knock on the door. "You got a phone call, said it's urgent, or I wouldn't have bothered. You gettin' anywhere with this punk yet?"

"No, but this better be important. This is the best shot we've had to bust this thing wide open. He'll talk sooner or later. What choice does he have?"

As the door closed, Patrick said in a whisper, "Oh, I'll talk all right. You better believe I will. It's gonna be a show-and-tell you won't believe."

It wasn't five minutes later that the detective returned, his face void of color.

"OK, I don't like it, but you're free to go."

"What do you mean, free to go?'

"What I said, you stupid or something? Get outta here, go. And take your two friends with you."

"You mean Robert and Richard are also being let go?"

"Yeah, that's what I mean, but stay available. We may have some questions. Don't leave the country or nothing."

"Yes sir. We'll be in the city. Easy to find. Thank you sir." Patrick insisted on a handshake from the officer as he left the room.

Robert and Richard were waiting in the lobby of the stationhouse, dumfounded, with huge grins on their faces.

Once outside, Richard was beside himself with joy, hugging Patrick. "I don't know what the hell you did kid, but I'm sorry I ever doubted you. Robert was right, you're terrific. I love ya!" Then, turning to Robert who was walking behind them. "What do you think, Robert, isn't he something? Why are you so quiet, say something, for crying out loud."

"And a child shall lead them." Robert said grinning from ear to ear.

143

CHAPTER THIRTY

"Let's see how fast we can get the hell out of here." Robert said to Richard and Patrick when they got back to the, not so, "Cozy Cabins."

"Wait a minute. Don't you want to hear what Patrick has to say? How he got us out?" Richard asked. "I'm dying to know."

"Not here fellows." Patrick said heading to his room "Trust me. I'll tell you everything in the car. The sooner we're outta here the better off we'll all be."

Fifteen minutes later they pulled onto Route 27 heading west to the City. There wasn't much to pack save their clothes and some personal effects as the police had confiscated everything that they thought might have anything to do with the movie company.

The equipment and truck rental companies on hearing the news on the radio, had immediately sent men to pick up their property. The police, having thoroughly gone over every truck, car, and piece of movie equipment, released the property.

The security men had gotten out of town before Ziggey got to the airport. However, finger prints lifted from the trucks would later reveal the unsavory past of some of them. Figuring that these guys were small fry they could always get later, all attention had focused on who they believed was the brains of the operation.

"Be a cold day in hell before I come back here." Robert said, obviously delighted and relieved to be leaving a place, an hour ago he wasn't so sure he'd ever leave.

"Don't be so sure." Patrick said with a smile.

"You gotta be kidding? Back here? Come on, out with it. You teased us long enough. Just what the hell did you do? No one can hear us now." Robert replied.

Savoring the moment, Patrick was about to tell the biggest story of his young life to a very appreciative audience.

"OK, guys you ready? You're not going to believe this, but trust me, it's all true. Do you want to stop for some coffee in Bridgehampton?"

"No, damit! Please get on with it. You're killing me." Robert said knowing that the kid was playing this for all it was worth.

"OK, OK. I'll start at the beginning. I don't know if either of you knew this or not, but I took my mini-cam with me. I figured I would use it to document the making of my first feature film. Something I could use as a promotional piece to get me more work or an agent."

Both Richard and Robert silently acknowledged the wisdom of this by nodding their heads.

"You probably thought I was either a snob or just a jerk when I kept refusing invitations to all the parties Ziggey was throwing and turning down all your invitations to go to diner or drinking with you guys, always saying I had to work on the script. Not so. You have no idea how much I wanted to party, hang out with you guys, but I figured this was an opportunity I shouldn't pass up. I was out shooting video tape every night. Sometimes only a half hour, other nights as much as two hours.

"Well, I got more than I bargained for. A hell of a lot more. There's some shit going on in this town after dark that nobody knows about...Well, they will now, or soon. Near as we can figure..."

"Wait a minute." Robert interrupted, What do you mean by 'we?' Who's the 'we?'"

"I was leading up to that. Give me a chance for a little drama, please. OK, I'll tell you. Then, I want to go back to the series of events as they unfolded, all right?"

"Fine. Who?" Robert agreed.

"The 'we' is Mr. Cohen and the law firm of Cohen, Feinberg, Grady, and Schwartz."

"Not Mr. Cohen, as in the father of Tiffany Cohen, is it?" Robert exclaimed.

"The very same. Now let me go on. You're gonna love this. So, I'm shooting every night. First few nights nothing unusual, I shot the same locations we did during the day figuring I'd add a voice track explaining why we did what we did and how I chose to shoot it. Well this wasn't very satisfactory with the limited lighting I had available so I started shooting during the day also. You probably didn't pay much attention. Probably just figured I was using the mini to set shots for the 35-millimeter camera.

"Anyway, things took an interesting turn the middle of the first week. I'm seeing all kinds of meetings going on in the most unlikely places. One, two, sometimes three in the morning these guys are talking in the alley behind that Pub off Main Street, another night in the parking lot behind the Barefoot Contessa. All over town in back alleys. One night I followed them to the Village dump. It was easy, they must have figured at that hour they were completely safe. Anyway, none of this makes any sense to me, but I figured something wasn't Kosher here. Something's going on that nobody is supposed to know about. Then one night, one guy hands over a big wad of cash. It wasn't wrapped or anything, just as plain as day. So, I figure it's a payoff of some kind, but I still don't know who these guys are."

"I can only assume, you do now." Robert asked proud of his protégée.

"I sure do. So do you. Wait, the best is yet to come. One of the guys is that nasty, wiseguy detective that arrested me. In it up to his ass. But I'm getting ahead of myself. The first few nights I didn't even view the tapes. I was too busy planning the next days shooting. Then I couldn't stand it any longer, and not only watched the tapes, but made some stills of the actors in this late night production. Then I went to the "East Hampton Star" asking if I could look at their morgue book of local citizens. Pow! As I said, our friend the cop, a member of the City Council and a State Senator seemed to be the principals. There were some others from time to time, but no one I could identify. We think they're out of state contractors. Cohen and company are working on that now."

"Sounds to me like you got some big time corruption scheme." Robert said. "What did you plan to do with this stuff?"

"Didn't know exactly what at the time. But I knew I had something with potential value."

Richard just sat there with his mouth open. His years of Ivory Tower academia had sheltered him from the real world so long, he felt this stuff only went on in the movies and an occasional incident in some rural community.

"Well we got something for sure. But that's only part of the story. I got the goods on our friend Ziggey as well. How do you think I got you guys outta the slammer?"

"I can't wait to hear." Robert said warming to the coming revelation.

"I gotta back up a little to keep things in sequence." Patrick went on. "The last day of filming, actually that night, when you had the wrap party, I did my usual. I was hoping these guys had another rendezvous, and I could get close-ups of some of the others. It was early so I didn't hold out much hope. As I told you, they usually met very late at night. So, I just shot some miscellaneous stuff. Stuff that I wanted for my promotion reel. Remember, I still thought I was directing a legitimate movie.

"Thinking I should go to the party to thank everyone, I finished shooting and headed there about nine thirty. I had left my car in the restaurant parking lot, as I was going to shoot around there anyway. I would put my camera in the trunk and have some fun for a change. However, as you may remember, I never made it to the party.

"Walking back through the city parking lot behind the grocery store across from the Laundry my eye caught what I assumed was the rays of a flashlight wildly playing off the walls inside. I thought maybe it was a burglar. So I crept up to a window, camera ready. I couldn't see faces at first, but there was a hell of a fight going on. One guy was trying to hit the other with the flashlight. He took a swing that illuminated the other guys face. Guess who? Never mind. I'll tell you. It was our cop friend. Anyway, the guy missed and the cop took out his gun and shot him. Don't know if he killed him or not, but I didn't stay around to find out.

"If this guy saw me I was dead meat, so I got outta there as fast as I could, got in my car and drove like hell to the city. Passed right by our motel and didn't stop till I got to my friend David's apartment on Bank Street in the Village.

"He's got some pretty sophisticated equipment and I wanted to view this stuff as soon as possible. Next morning when I heard the news, I knew they'd be looking for me, so I stayed with him. Matter of fact, you might even know him. He's a waiter at Jimmy's, in his last year of NYU Film School. We were roommates my last year.

"When David hears the whole story, I told him about you guys, how good you were to me, and how the news said you were busted...it was like a light bulb went off in his head."

"'I can help!' He sez. 'At least I think I can?'

"'What'd you mean?' I asked. 'How can you help? Help with what?" But he's ignoring me while futzing around with his computer. 'I think I may have something on my hard drive that may interest you.' He says.

"He's one of those computer nuts, probably doesn't take a crap without entering it on bowel movement chart. Anyway, he's adjusting the screen while I'm switching to CNN to see if we made the national news wires when he yells out. 'Got it! I thought I'd saved it, but wasn't sure.'

"'You save everything don't you?' I asked, still having no idea what 'it' was.

"'You won't laugh at me anymore, Mr. Big Shot Director. I just saved your ass and your friends as well, so cut the crap and come take a look.' He said as he turned on his printer.

"What I saw blew my mind, as it will yours, Gentlemen."

"Will you please get to the point. Enough with the melodrama, you're killin' me." Robert said. Richard still had his mouth open.

"OK, you won't believe this, actually now you will, but I didn't understand it at first. Your friend Ziggey, if that's his real name, asked my friend David to make a printout from a three and a half inch floppy disc. Gave him some cock and bull story about some European movie deal he was putting together. Thing is, he didn't want David to see on what was on the disc. David went along with it figuring this guy was some big deal and maybe he would give him a job when he finished school. Little did he know."

"Will you please get to the point before I collect my first social security check. Your beginning to sound like a God damn writer." Robert said with his hands lightly around Patrick's neck. Richard's mouth had closed only slightly.

Patrick was obviously enjoying this moment in the sun.

"On the screen was twenty pages of personal information about the houses and personal habits of some of the families in East Hampton. I mean complete information. The kinds of cars they drove, license plate numbers, the length of time they spent in East Hampton, the maid, pool guy and gardeners schedules, and, get this, the combination to their safes, and in one house, instructions to enter a walk-in vault.

"We don't know where he got this information yet, but Mr. Cohen turned it over the D.A.'s office in the city figuring they'll come up with something soon. How's that grab you?"

"I'm impressed. I didn't think the short Mr. Z had the tenacity for research." Robert said. "So what'd you do next?"

"I really wasn't sure what to do, but I knew you were dating the daughter of some rich lawyer."

"How'd you know that? Don't tell me. You got us on tape?" Robert asked only half-seriously.

"No, but everybody knew it. You were never in your room, at least not overnight. It wasn't too hard to figure you had some chick somewhere, so we looked until we got the answer. Very lovely, I might add."

"Thanks for you vote of confidence in my choice of, as you so delicately put it, some chick." Robert smiled.

"Sorry about that. Guess I fail Politically Correct 101? Anyway, fortunately for all of us, I remembered where she lived, and checked my videotapes. I knew I had shot her family's house, and as fate would have it, they have a very prominent name plate on their mailbox. So I called her, she called her father, her father called me at David's and we did lunch. Then your lovely young lady visited you in the slammer, came to the city and we all did dinner at the Beatrice Inn in the village. Assume you guys know the place?"

"Yea, yea, we know." Replied a frustrated Robert "Been going there since before you were born."

"Would be a great place for a wrap party." Patrick replied, still milking his moment.

"Will you *please* just get on with it before I strangle you." Robert said reaching for his throat.

"I still don't get it though. Granted the information sheets would nail Ziggey, but what convinced them that we weren't part of it?" Robert asked.

"Easy. You guys couldn't have been involved. You were the most visible people in town. People could attest to seeing you almost every minute of every day, and certainly the night of the burglaries. And they bought the fact that we were all duped.

"Richard was the first one at the party and the last to leave. And even though you were with the ever-lovely Tiffany, her support of your alibi was good enough for the police. Although I think daddy's a little pissed that his daughter just might not be a virgin anymore."

"She is." Robert said with a smile.

"She is? ...What?" Patrick asked incredulous.

"She is lovely." Robert laughed.

CHAPTER THIRTY-ONE

The last two weeks had been the busiest, most exciting, and most rewarding in Patrick's young life.

The law firm of Cohen, Feinberg, Grady and Schwartz provided office space, an editing room, and whatever personnel and supplies Patrick, Robert and Richard might need to edit Patrick's videotape. Along with the finished tape, they were to prepare a written account of their experience with Ziggey.

In addition to the video, they had nine days of unedited thirty-five millimeter film footage to take a hard look at. The film was at a processing lab in the city. The tenth and last day of film had been confiscated by the local police and was still in East Hampton.

Even though released by the police, these three were not out of hot water and still might be indicted on very superficial evidence. This was one angry, raped town. They had to nail somebody and there were those who simply didn't care how good their alibis were. They didn't buy the fact that one man could have done all this alone. He had to have accomplices and Richard, Robert and Patrick were the most likely. They had the same access to homes and property as Ziggey, so they reasoned that they were involved in setting the stage for the break-ins.

The firm at the behest of Mr. Cohen had taken them on pro bono. It was to be his baby, though. There were those in the company not thrilled about representing a case of such notoriety. But for Mr. Cohen these three characters were a colorful diversion. And, of course, to placate the lovely Tiffany. Not that the firm didn't stand to profit from the positive press if these clients were proved innocent.

After rough cuts of both video and film had been assembled the authorities were called in for viewing. The hope was that the material would reveal some telling evidence about Ziggey. Stranger things have happened. Maybe someone was caught on the film or the tape that didn't belong. Someone in a crowd scene maybe? Anyway, it was worth a shot. This cooperation also helped to establish the innocence of the three.

"Stop the film!" An FBI agent yelled. "I think I recognized someone. Can you run it back a few feet, then run it in slow motion?"

Patrick stopped the projector. "Just a second. I can do all that, plus give you freeze-framing and enhanced close-ups on the video tape copy I made. Whatever you like. How far back you want me to go?"

"To the beginning of that crowd scene on, it looked like Main Street."

"It was Main Street. I remember the scene. Terrible day. It rained like hell." Patrick said as he rewound.

"That's it. Start there in slow motion please."

"You got it."

"Not yet, not yet." The agent said leaning forward, intent on the screen. Wait! Hold it! Stop! That's him. I think? Zoom in. Can you enlarge with this thing? If not, I'll have to take the film to our lab. We can do it there."

"No sweat. Mr. Cohen let me buy the best. Anything you want." Patrick said already zooming in on the face in question. "This the guy you mean?"

"Yeah, that's him. I'm sure I know him."

"Him?" Patrick said laughing. "He's just another pretty actor. He was a jerk. A real pain in the ass."

"What do you mean? How was he a pain in the ass? Tell me all you know about him. Did you hire him? How'd he come to be in the picture? Anything you can think of might help me." Said the agitated agent.

Patrick looked at Richard.

"I cast him." Richard timidly said.

"Then you tell me. Where did you find him? Did you call him or what? I don't know how you guys work."

"Well." Richard said, trying to remember. "It was weeks ago when I did the casting. I got a call from this guy's agent in Hollywood."

"Go on. He's from California then? What's his name?"

"I don't know where he's from. Nobody is actually from California. His name? I forget, but I could look it up on the call sheet."

Patrick and Robert both had their call sheets out looking.

"Gary. Gary Gordon." said Robert.

"Yeah, that's it." Patrick chimed in. "Real jerk. I can't believe he had anything to do with Ziggey. Two guys couldn't be more different. And for sure he isn't smart enough to pull off anything like what happened."

"You'd be surprised, young fellow, just who's capable of what. You said he's an actor. Well, consider this, maybe he was just acting dumb? Anyway, go on Richard. I still can't place him. You said his agent called you from Hollywood. You don't happen to have a resumé do you? Wait a minute, don't these actors always give you one of those glossy pictures? If you have one, I'd like that too."

"Yes. Somewhere. It's in my office. I'll be right back." Richard said, happy to be able to get away from this interrogation for a moment or two. Was he somehow, inadvertently, responsible for hiring a felon? Was this going to weaken his defense? Would he be accused again of complicity?

Patrick, you keep saying he was a jerk, a pain in the ass. How so?"

"He was always underfoot. Like a kid with his first part. He kept asking if I couldn't find a way to expand his role. Give him more lines, more camera time."

"Me too." Robert added. "He kept bugging me to write more for him, another scene, anything. Seems this was his comeback. Richard told me he'd been a big daytime soap star years ago, then dropped out."

"That's it! I know who the son of bitch is now."

"Who?" Richard asked entering the room not sure he wanted to know.

"The minute you said daytime soap actor, it came back. We've been trying to get something on him for years. Something that a D.A. could take to a Grand Jury. I'll tell you this for sure. He ain't no dummy. He's the smartest and slipperiest fence this department has come across in years."

Everybody's mouth was now open.

"We know what he's fenced, and in most cases where he's fenced it. But we've always been one step behind. He's international. Everybody wants a piece of this guy including Interpol. He slips in and out of this country like a submarine. Acting, my foot! He's in this up to his neck with your Mr. Z. Now to find the elusive bastard. Thanks guys. You've been a big help. OK, if I take the picture and resumé with me?" The agent asked, already at the door.

The agent gone, they resumed the show for the remaining authorities. This too proved successful. From Patrick's video they were able to identify the state senator, and one of the other men. The detective that had arrested Patrick was under twenty-four hour surveillance.

A week later, the District Attorneys' office had put together a complete package of indictments that stretched from East Hampton, through New York City, all the way up to Albany.

It was the biggest case of political corruption in the history of the state. There wasn't a state road, state building, school or park built or repaired in the last ten years that this crowd didn't profit from.

Everyone was happy. The feds were thrilled with getting a line on one of their most wanted. The sophistication of the operation and those involved, convinced them that Robert, Richard and Patrick had been duped.

The state police were similarly grateful for their help. Not only with the corruption case, but a pending indictment against Yoshi who was being questioned as the source of Ziggey's dossiers.

The one thread that tied all the victimized homes together was that at one time or another they all had common business interests with Yoshi.

Life was beautiful for the exonerated trio as the name of their newly formed production company was stenciled on the entrance to their suite of new offices: "R.P.R. Film Productions. A Joint Venture of Cohen, Feinberg, Grady and Schwartz." There's hardly a lawyer alive that doesn't want to get into show business one way or the other.

Their first production was almost complete. A feature length docu-drama melding footage from the film they shot for the feature with Patrick's video recordings. Robert was writing additional scenes needed to flush it out along with a voice over narrative where needed. Richard would play the state senator. Directed, of course, by Patrick.

CHAPTER THIRTY-TWO

The past few weeks saw Ziggey spending money like the drunk he was fast becoming, albeit, on a better quality of booze than he was used to. He was trying to emulate the lifestyle of the rich people of East Hampton and others he'd seen in the movies. He bought a car, a thirty-foot cabin cruiser, and had his clothes made to order. His money was being depleted in large chunks, but it didn't bother him, he had millions of dollars in paintings to support his philandering. Gary would come through, then he would decide what to do with the rest of his life. Maybe move to Europe or South America to continue the good life.

Ziggey walked into his favorite restaurant's cocktail lounge at quarter to noon as he had done every day for the past two weeks.

"Good afternoon, Mr. Wilson. Nice to see you. Hope you had a good nights sleep." Slobbered the Matre'D.

"Yes, Maxwell, I did. Thanks for asking." Ziggey answered making his way to the bar.

"Make another million on the market yesterday, sir?" Maxwell called after him.

Laughing, Ziggey turned. "No, afraid not, Max. Bad day, looks like only a half a mill."

Seeing Ziggey approach, the bartender leaned over to a customer. "I'm sorry sir, but you'll have to move. You're in Mr. Wilson's seat."

"Who the hell is Mr. Wilson?" The burly customer asked belligerently. "He can sit somewhere else. I ain't movin'."

"That's not true, sir." Said the bartender raising his hand in a signal.

A minute later the bartender, with the help of two security men, roughly escorted the drunk past Ziggey to the door. "Be with you in sec. Mr. Wilson." The bartender said to Ziggey as they passed him.

"No sweat, Charlie." Ziggey said sitting down. No sooner did he land on his seat than a crowd of his new friends surrounded him. The bartender on his return asked, as he did every day, "The usual for you and your friends, Mr. Wilson?"

"Set 'em up." Ziggey said throwing a hundred dollar bill on the bar amid the usual back-slapping and wise-cracking among his groupies.

After serving the drinks Charlie turned on the TV over the bar to the noon CNN news. It was just beginning.

"We have this breaking story just in." said the anchor man. "The FBI in Los Angeles has just arrested a man they believe to have been involved in what has been called the "Great Movie Robbery" case in East Hampton, New York. The man, who gave his name as..."

"Hey, turn it up will you, Charlie." Asked one of Ziggey's buddies. "I want to hear this, I got a friend in East Hampton, that got robbed. I sure hope they nail that bastard."

Ziggey had been too busy impressing a young woman to have paid any attention to the news until the volume was turned up just as the anchorman said,

"... Gary Gordon, was taken into custody last night after an exhaustive search." This got his attention as he pushed the woman away to concentrate.

"Hey what's the problem?" She asked. "Since when have you been so interested in the news?"

"Gary Gordon, one of the many aliases used by him, has been sought as a high-class fence in many burglaries over the last five years."

"Glad they finally got what looks like a good lead." said the other interested party at the bar. "Maybe my friend will get some of his stuff back now? Terrible thing what's happening in the States now, don't you agree? Ralph."

"Uh, yeah sure. Terrible. You can't trust nobody, no more." Ziggey said, trying to listen without seeming too interested.

His mind was racing with thoughts of the possible ramifications of Gary's arrest. Will he talk to save his own ass? Will the son of a bitch give me up? Will he tell 'em about the stolen art to cut a deal? Shit, he knows where I am, what my name is, everything.

Ziggey ordered a double Chivas Regal which he sipped till the end of the half hour news cast. Not wanting to arouse suspicions he excused himself, saying he had to make a phone call. Returning to the bar, after the make believe phone call he said, "Listen, I gotta go guys. Sorry, but something just came up back in the States that I gotta attend to right away or it could cost me a fortune."

"You OK, Mr. Wilson?" Charlie asked. "You look kinda pale."

"No, I'm fine. Here Charlie," he said throwing another hundred on the bar. "Buy everyone another round. Keep the change."

Some were surprised at the sudden departure, but it wasn't the first time he had left them alone at this noontime ritual. They figured that he was a little eccentric, and as in the past, he would show up later to shoot pool or play poker like they did every day.

Not today. Ziggey was in trouble and he knew it. He had to execute his departure earlier than he had planned. Of

159

course Gary would give him up, he thought as he entered his room. He had to. Anything he could do to cut a deal for himself. I'd do the same thing in a New York minute. I gotta get the hell outta here and now, he concluded as he started to pack.

His hands were shaking and he had a splitting headache, as he pulled cash out of hiding places. How much time do I have? If the Feds were telling the truth, that they arrested him last night, how soon will the bastards be here?

He kept looking out the window. Were there any strangers around? Guys with suits and ties. He could see the Marina where his boat was docked. No one around that. At least not yet.

"Don't panic, you got it worked out, try and relax." He said, pacing frantically around his suite.

"Shit, I got something they'll kill for. Even if they get me, which they ain't, I'll walk. Hell, I'll plea bargain my ass down to a Jay Walking ticket. Why didn't I think of it sooner. No way Gary is gonna use those paintings to save his ass. And screw Yoshi. My ass is on the line now."

One bag of clothes was all he would need. He wanted to leave as much in the room as possible so when they came, and he knew they would, it would look like he was coming back. It would buy him some necessary time.

Leaving the hotel by a staircase so as not to be seen in the lobby, he walked the backstreets to his boat. He dropped off his clothes and put most of the cash that was bulging his pockets into a small wall safe. He still had the bag of unset diamonds in his pocket that he figured would keep him a long time.

He looked at his watch, it was one in the afternoon. He was very nervous. "They still better be there." He said now running through sidestreet to the bank. "What if the Feds called the bank? What if Mrs. Yoshi heard the news and called the banker?"

160

More causes for anxiety. "Please God. Just one more bit of luck and I'm home free." He pleaded.

As casually as he could under the circumstances, Ziggey strolled into the bank. Nothing looked unusual as he requested entry to the vault and signed the log book.

"So far so good." He whispered, as he was led to the vault, craning his neck to see if he was followed. Finally left alone he opened his box. The paintings were as he left them, in a sealed cardboard box that gave no clue as to the contents.

"Thank you very much." He said to the clerk. "I need to check a few papers in here. Bring it back tomorrow." He wanted everything to look normal.

Leaving the bank, he checked in every direction. No one suspicious as far as he could tell.

Again through sidestreets to the Marina. He stopped out of sight of his boat and waited a few minutes to see if anything untoward was going on.

Nothing. At least nothing apparent.

"Looks like you pulled it off again." He said, relaxing a little as he boarded his cruiser and made a thorough search.

"Now to get the fuck outta here." He said, starting the engine.

"Gonna do a little fishing?" Someone asked from a neighboring boat.

It startled the hell out of Ziggey, but then he recognized the party. "Uh, yeah. You got it. I heard the marlin are runnin'. Just got a call. See ya."

Ziggey had no idea what a marlin was or if they ran. It was an expression he'd heard. But maybe it was accurate. His neighbor didn't react so he guessed he said the right thing. He was amused and pleased with the cleverness of his remark.

Ziggey left the harbor slowly. No police boats, no Coast Guard. "Damned if I didn't make it." He said, proud of his escape.

Once out of the harbor, he gunned the boat. Not the time to get smug. He had to get where he was going quickly and execute the rest of his plan. The Feds could be landing at Bimini airport right now.

Looking at a chart, he pointed to a barely discernible dot. "That's it. Something, Cay. An island of less than twenty inhabitants. They'll never find me. I'll own it."

After only a few minutes at high speed, Ziggey pulled next to a decrepit dock, on what appeared to be a deserted island. "Just like I planned. Just sooner than I expected."

Ziggey had cruised the waters frequently looking for just this place. He had made arrangements here to live a very modest life with the millions from the painting sale until the heat died down. When he felt it was safe, he would make his way to South America, and maybe Europe from there.

Tied at this rickety dock he scanned the horizon for any sign of danger. Then the sky. He could have been followed by air. Satisfied he went below to get his money, the box of paintings, a battery operated TV, an AM FM radio with a police band, and a few other necessities.

Walking inland about a five hundred yards he arrived in what passed for a town. A general store that also served as a bar, restaurant, and place where you could by gas in five gallon cans. This was the whole town. There were no cars on this island, but a few people had motor bikes, and occasionally a boat would stop by in desperate need of enough fuel to get to a bigger port.

At the store he bought some canned goods, several bottles of Scotch, some week old newspapers from the states, and a five gallon can of gas. "Looks like you plan to stay with us for a while this time?" The proprietor said.

"Yeah, I think so. Life has gotten a little to hectic for me. Need to chill out for a while. You know, smell the coffee beans.   See ya later." He said, leaving with his supplies.

Ziggey then walked about another five hundred yards to a tin-roofed shack on the other side of this small island.

"Not so bad."   Ziggey said surveying his new home. "Could be worse. I could be in the slammer, and this time it wouldn't be one of those country club joints. "You done good." He said, talking to himself. "A coupla months in this dump, and I'll be back livin' the good life.   Take these paintings and sell 'em myself in South America. What'd I need that creep for anyway?"

He poured himself a large glass of Scotch and raised it in a toast and said looking into a dingy mirror. "To the "Z" man. The greatest con man of all time."

After drinking half the bottle he fell asleep on the single bed. When he woke it was dark. Going outside he inhaled the fresh air and looked for anything suspicious. Nothing. He was very pleased with himself, returning to the cabin.

Gonna be a little lonely, but what the hell, I got my TV and those newspapers to read. Hell, maybe I'll even write my memories. Should be worth a fortune to some movie company.

"Let's see what they get on TV in this dump. Probably just some island crap." He said, pouring another drink. To his surprise he found out that he got stations from Miami, and Puerto Rico. "Not bad. I'll survive. Just like I always do."

He emptied a can of beans into a pot, turned on the gas, made another drink, and settled down to watch the movie that was on his small set.

"And now for the early evening news from the South Land. Then back to our movie. Our lead story tonight concerns that infamous robbery up north known as the "Great Movie Robbery."

"Jesus, what now?" Ziggey yelled. "Wait a minute what've I got to worry about? Nobody's gonna find me here."

"Although the police made no connection at first, there is evidence that the escape, yesterday, of Yamamoto Yoshi from Federal Authorities has something to do with that case.

"He made good his escape while being transported to the New York City's District Attorneys' office to be questioned in connection with information given to the police from Gary Gordon who the FBI arrested yesterday in Los Angeles. Conjecture is that Mr. Yoshi was the third part of the triangle that masterminded this case. It has been revealed that, Mr. Zignorelli, the man who actually committed the burglaries, was a friend of Mr. Yoshi while serving time with him in the Connecticut facility.

"Police were convinced from the start that there had to be someone with sophistication and brain power sorely lacking in Mr. Zignorelli. No way they said, 'could a little two-bit punk like him pull off a crime of this magnitude without help, let alone plan it.'"

"Little two-bit punk, Huh!" Ziggey screamed at the TV. Sorely lacking my ass! It was me! All me! That little Jap bastard had no idea what I was going to do, or how I did it till after it was over. Fuck you!"

"We now have all the players identified." Said a police spokesman. "And as soon as we get Yoshi, we're sure he'll be only to happy to lead us to Zignorelli."

"More on this breaking story as we get details. Now for local news."

Ziggey was so mad at not getting the credit for being the mastermind of America's greatest robbery, that the significance of Yoshi's escape temporarily eluded him.

Angrily, he turned off the TV, drank a glass of Scotch then another before it hit him.

"Shit! He's after me and his fucking paintings!" he yelled at the mirror. Again panic. "Yoshi's no dummy.

164

He's got connections I don't want to know about. He'd find me long before the Feds. I know for sure he's got connections in Bimini, the banker for one, and who knows who else. I better get further away." He said, pouring a third drink and dropping dejectedly into a chair.

"I gotta come up with something, and fast." His eye caught sight of the five gallon gas can, at the same time a light bulb went off in his head.

"That's it!" he said bolting out of the chair. "It's simple and these people here will back me up. Perfect! And they think I ain't smart. I'll show them. They ain't never gonna get the "Z" man."

Grabbing the gas can he hurried to his boat. It was pitch-black out, no moon, all the better for his plan. On board, he strategically placed some of his clothing both above and below decks in the bow sections of the boat wrapping several items in kapok life preservers. He then went to the stern, opened the engine compartment covers splashing gasoline all over the cavity. Then, soaking a ten foot piece of line with gas, he placed one end in the still half-full gas can that he placed next to the engine, and draped the other end over the stern lying it on the shore.

Then he went into the cockpit and tied the wheel in such a way that the boat would make a straight course. Pushing the throttle to high he started the engine in neutral. He then tied a long length of coiled line to the shift lever and left the boat with the engine racing in neutral.

On the dock he untied the fore and aft lines holding the boat maintaining control with the coiled line in his hand. At the stern he lit the ten foot section of line that served as a fuse. He waited until the fuse crossed from shore to the stern of the boat, then yanked hard on his coiled rope, putting the engine in gear. Immediately the boat raced out to sea pulling Ziggey on his face into the water.

He let go after a few feet, then stood watching and pleading with God. It seemed like an eternity had gone by

165

before anything happened. A series of explosions lit up the dark sky and black water like the biggest Fourth of July fireworks display he'd ever seen.

"It worked." He said pleased with himself once again. "I'm dead. The 'Z' man is dead, but never forgotten."

EPILOGUE

It had been six very long months since the pronouncement of Ziggey's death. Some of the clothing he had carefully placed in the bow of the boat survived and were identified. Most law enforcement officials bought his death. Some didn't. But since the stolen property in Gary Gordon's possession was returned, the case was marked closed in most quarters. Others placed it in an inactive file.

Reduced to being just another "little punk" by the police and media, the bearded, disheveled Ziggey, was despondent. Sick with boredom, running low on money, (buying and maintaining his neighbors silence was more costly than he thought), reduced to drinking rot-gut whiskey, he didn't even have his pride left. He knew what he had done, but would never get the credit or be revered for it. No one would ever believe him to be the genius he was.

So he languished in his one-room shanty, ludicrously decorated with millions of dollars in art that, of course, had not been reported stolen, even though Gary did try to tell the police that he could lead them to a fortune in stolen art. When the police questioned the owner of that house, he denied owning any such paintings, saying that what he had were some quality reproductions of the masters valued at only several hundred dollars each. They weren't even insured, so not to worry. The elaborate vault was for storage of his wife's furs, and some valuable antiques and jewelry when they would be away for a long period.

Only three people knew about the art, four counting Ziggey. One, the victim, who couldn't talk, the second,

Gary, who no one believed, and Yoshi. Yoshi was a constant cause for concern.

Ziggey spent most of his waking hours surveying the horizon and shore lines. Every boat, every low flying plane, every fisherman stopping for supplies, was cause for great paranoia. His life was hell, with thoughts of suicide in recurring nightmares and daylight stupors.

Once a month, the owner of the general store would drop an assortment of old newspapers and magazines from the States on Ziggey's porch. No one was allowed inside, not that anyone ever wanted entrance.

Finally a ray of hope. A reprieve. In a month old U. S. News and World Report the following story buoyed his spirits.

"Escaped Federal fugitive, Yamamoto Yoshi killed in a drug raid in Los Angeles. It seems Mr. Yoshi, a business executive and a sought after Federal escapee, was hiding out in a run down section of South Central, L. A. in what police believed to be the distribution point of a large drug operation. Mr. Yoshi had been a member of this gang as a youth. He and several members of the gang were killed in what police described as the most ferocious gun battle in the last decade.

"Along with the huge quantities of drugs, cash, and guns, police found a detailed map of the island of Bimini and the Cay Islands on one of the dead men. Police plan to follow up on this lead, believing that area as a possible interim stop on the drug route."

The relief of the headline news, was short-lived. Obviously, Yoshi had hired this guy to kill him and get the paintings. What survivor of this gang might still be hunting him? And the police will start nosing around again. There would be no peace.

The production company of R. P. & R., had just finished filming "The Two Sides of a Wealthy Community" and were celebrating with a weekend cruise on a party boat off the

168

coast of Bimini. This area had been their last location. The last known residence of a super con man.

The docu-drama explored the life of corrupt small town officials, and the life style of a wealthy community of part-time residents that took no notice.

Included was an examination of how even the most sophisticated could easily be conned by a clever criminal. Ziggey would never see the credit he got for being the mastermind of this famous con.

Ziggey's car had been found, then the helicopter pilot had been interviewed. From there it was easy. The time of Ziggey's car rental coincided with the time the pilot said he dropped him off. It was the only car rented at that hour at Westchester County Airport.

The car was traced to Newark Airport. Flight departure schedules were checked. Photos of Ziggey were enhanced making him taller, then fatter, then with hair, and circulated to airport and flight personal.

He was identified. The rest was easy. The charter pilot that took him from Puerto Rico to Bimini had dutifully logged his flight with air traffic control. He remembered the disagreeable passenger that didn't talk, but threw up all over the cockpit.

Ralph Wilson was identified as Ziggey. Charlie the bartender and Ziggey's "friends" all thought "there was something fishy about that guy."

While everyone onboard was having a good time eating, drinking and dancing, Patrick, never without some kind of camera, was on the flying bridge taking still shots through a telephoto lens.

Looking through the lens he suddenly yelled, "Holy shit! I don't believe it. It can't be." Then looking away he wiped his eyes and looked back through the lens.

"Robert! Richard! Stop the boat! Come up here! You're not going to believe this! I'm not sure I do."

When they got on the bridge, fearing they were sinking or something equally dramatic, Patrick pulled both of them to his camera. "Here look through the lens. Tell me what you see. Tell me I'm not hallucinating. Is that who I think it is?"

Richard looked, then Robert. Then they looked at each other in disbelief. Then both to Patrick saying in unison, "Yup, it's him all right. Needs a shave and a haircut, but it's him all right."

After a brief, reflective pause, each silently staring at the other, Robert finally saying, "Somehow or other I didn't buy his death."

"Well you could fool me, he sure doesn't look so good from here." Patrick said laughing.

"I'm sure he's gonna surface somehow, somewhere. Wonder what he'll come back as?" Richard chimed in. "I doubt as a movie producer, but who knows with him?"

Patrick still laughing, "We could have a new ending for our film or the start of a new one: "Con Man Resurrected."

CPSIA information can be obtained
at www.ICGtesting.com
Printed in the USA
FSOW04n1357220617
35493FS